There Goes M

by

L.L. Dahlin

This is a work of fiction. Names, characters, places, and incidents are either the product of the author's imagination or are used fictitiously, and any resemblance to actual persons living or dead, business establishments, events, or locales, is entirely coincidental.

There Goes My Bailey

COPYRIGHT © 2018 by L.L. Dahlin

All rights reserved. No part of this book may be used or reproduced in any manner whatsoever without written permission of the author except in the case of brief quotations embodied in critical articles or reviews.

Published by L.L. Dahlin
Edited by Tee Tate
Cover Art by Karrie Jax
Publishing History
First Edition, 2018
Digital ISBN 978-0998479590
Print ISBN 978-1980697473

Published in the United States of America

Dedication

Tessa – I've followed your author journey since the very beginning and have been blown away by your stories and your characters. After meeting you I was impressed by your positivity and willingness to help a fellow author. Your ability to take a picture and make a mini synopsis with it is what made me bring you one of my very favorite pictures to look at. I wanted to see if I could take your words and spin them into a story. Thank you for all you do with your fans and authors who are also fans. I can't wait to see where your journey leads you.

Thank you, also, for introducing me to Harold Bailey.

Acknowledgements

The women who support me in this journey come from a wide range of experiences. Some I know from face to face interactions and others I've never met in person, but my life is richer, fuller and more fulfilling because I know you. Thank you.

Angie D., Andy B., Jenny Ra., Jen Re., Camisha and Heather K,.

My amazing editor, Tee Tate, whose fixes and thoughtful incite helps to make my story richer. Hugs and thanks.

This list is woefully incomplete, because there are so many people to thank, and I appreciate each and every one of you. If you have purchased or were given a copy of this book, then consider yourself highly appreciated and a part of my journey.

Hugs, Love and Blessings to you all.

Chapter 1

"HAROLD BAILEY? WHAT the fuck are you doing here?" The man, who stood above him with his fist still balled up and bloodied from the punch that left him on the floor, had a voice that was deeper than he remembered it, but it still had the ability to make his cock perk up.

Bailey looked up into the face of the man who'd just did a hell of a multitasking job of trying to juggle an unruly bar patron and laying him flat on his ass at the same time. The truth was he hadn't been ready to see this man or to protect himself. He'd seen that his best friend's younger brother, Scott Callahan, was about to be in a fight and his mind flashed back to the times where people would pick on the small, pretty boy who had often needed saving. He'd come over to do what he'd done so many times before, but this time it wasn't needed. Scott was a lot bigger, stronger and more capable than he'd been back in the day. It was abundantly clear the man could take care of himself.

Now that Bailey was closer to the situation a few more things were noticeable. Like the fact that the younger man was probably security for the loud and lively sports bar and wasn't in danger at all. Scott kept his focus split between the original troublemaker and Bailey, but the customer had settled down quite a bit, probably hoping not to get his ass handed to him the way Bailey had. The funny thing is he'd taught Scott that technique and how to land that exact punch. Talk about things coming full circle. There were times when Harold Bailey felt like a fucking genius, but then there were times like this. Bailey couldn't remember the last time he was knocked on his ass. Mentally, yes, but physically? No. The feeling of falling to the ground as his face exploded with pain seemed to happen in slow motion. He looked up into the slightly changed face that he hadn't seen in about eight years and realized this guy was the deliverer of the last *mental* TKO he'd received as well.

The intense moment of seeing Scott again had ebbed a bit as his nose demanded more attention as it ached and throbbed. The same nose that his best friend's younger brother had just punched. He couldn't believe he'd run into fucking Scott Callahan, the biggest reason he'd hightailed it out of his hometown years ago, and the man responsible for his presence here tonight. Bailey was able to keep the carnage blocked with his two big hands as he got up from the floor, but he could feel the blood becoming too much to hold back.

"Go to the bathroom and take care of that. I'll see you when you get out." Scott's voice was gruff before he turned his back on him, taking his shocked, haunted eyes away from Bailey's view and escorting the rowdy man to the door.

Bailey wanted nothing more than to get his coat and leave the bar, but since he would probably have an issue getting a cab back to his hotel looking like he'd left the scene of a massacre, he figured cleaning up was the best idea for now. He wasn't sure what would be revealed when he moved his hands, but he didn't think it would be good.

Keeping a low profile was what he'd been going for as he sat at the bar, the loud music, contemporary furniture and huge televisions that couldn't be heard over said music, was filled with men. It wasn't hard to see why this place was in the directory of establishments that catered to men loving, men with a five out of 5-star rating. His low profile had been blown by his own ridiculousness. It seemed like the whole room followed him with their eyes as he walked quickly across the dimly lit floor to the bathroom. Apparently, it wasn't dim enough for them to miss him running over to save a bouncer that didn't need saving in the first place. When he finally made it to the brightly lit bathroom, he grabbed a few paper towels with one hand and quickly brought it to his face. Bailey didn't know if he was prepared to assess the damage to his pride, but figured it was better to concentrate on his nose instead of how much of a fool he'd just made of himself in front of all the patrons and the man who was his biggest regret.

Pressing the paper against his nose for a few minutes, he peeled it away to see if his nose was still bleeding. It wasn't as bad as he'd thought it'd be. His nose was swollen a little, but it wasn't broken. Bailey manipulated the bridge of his nose just to make sure his first assessment was correct. Damn. The pain made him hiss. He remembered teaching Scott how to throw a punch, but he never thought the guy had perfected the technique, or that he'd find out how good of a teacher he'd been in such an up close and personal way. Blood was no longer trickling out of his nose, so he wiped his face and took a good look at himself in the mirror.

"What the fuck *am* I doing here?" he asked his reflection, but the truth was he could have asked Scott the same thing. No one had told him that the man worked at The Male Box, just a few miles away from their hometown. This club catered to men who enjoyed men, but didn't really advertise itself as a gay bar. It was more like a sports bar, with everyone knowing the underlying features. Bailey shook his head and was glad that his nose had stopped bleeding. Now he had to work up to talking to Scott, and even after eight years, he wasn't ready. He didn't know how long he stood there after his face was clean, but he was in no hurry to leave the bathroom. Looking down at his clothes he was happy that at least he was able to keep the mess contained to his hands and face.

The door opened, and in walked the man Bailey'd simultaneously wanted to avoid and was working up the gonads to talk to. Who knew Scott would have changed from the boy who looked for help in a fight to one who could take care of himself. He studied his old friend in the mirror. Short, dark hair with just a little extra on top, like most of the recruits he'd seen in the last eight year years, a seven-thirty shadow, which was a little more than five o'clock shadow but less than a full beard. The look wasn't original at all, but somehow Scott made it different. His gaze slid to those lips that were pursed so tightly at this moment and wondered how they would feel like when they were relaxed and fitted against his. What would the hair on his face feel like scraping against his, or how would it feel against his tongue? Scott had gotten a little taller, and he'd grown a good deal of muscle. The awkward teen look was gone, and it had been replaced by a man who appeared confident in his skin and sure of his place in the world.

Bailey had known him since they were both young boys because Scott was his best friend Ollie's only sibling. They'd protected Ollie's kid brother from being targeted, mostly because the neighborhood kids thought he was different and meek. Scott wouldn't ever fight when he was bullied. The slim-built boy with his pretty face had grown up in his absence. Bailey let himself take in the way Scott filled out his clothes but noted his pretty face hadn't changed all that much. What had changed was now Scott was the man guarding the door and protecting others against bullies.

"Are you planning to come out of the bathroom?" Scott leaned next to the door like he didn't want to get too close, and that was fine with Bailey. He'd been studying the man's image in the mirror for so long it was almost surreal when Scott actually said something. Even after he'd been punched, it had taken a few seconds for his half chub to go away when he realized Scott was that close to him after all this time. It was a good thing Bailey favored loose-fitting pants because even with all this awkwardness, facial pain, and thick silence, his cock still wanted Scott to notice him.

"Yes." Bailey looked at the man in the mirror, fearing that if his friend's potency was this strong with indirect eye contact, looking directly into the clear amber eyes might do him in. "I'm just pulling myself together after getting clocked at the door."

"I'm sorry about that. I didn't know it was you. I assumed I was getting double teamed. In times of conflict, it can be detrimental to stop and ask questions." Scott paused but narrowed his eyes. "What made you jump in harm's way in the first place?"

"I saw you fighting that guy, realized who you were and came over—"

"To rescue me, right? Just like old times?"

Bailey nodded slightly and then chuckled a bit. "Doesn't look like you needed much assistance. Times have definitely changed."

"True. I'm a police officer now, but I come to The Male Box and do security for them part-time."

"I'd heard about the police thing, but I hadn't heard about this job."

"Yes, well, my brother doesn't know everything about me." Scott stepped away from the wall and walked closer to Bailey. "So why are you here again?"

"I'm just out of the military. I did eight years, but I did some damage to my arm and didn't want to re-up, so I'm home." Bailey still hadn't turned around, and now it felt weird as fuck just watching and talking to Scott by way of the mirror.

"I know that part. I'm supposed to see you at the dinner your folks are having for you tomorrow. You were supposed to be getting picked up by Ollie tomorrow afternoon at the airport. I'm aware of a lot of things." Scott put his hand on Bailey's shoulder and gently tugged so he'd spin around. "What I'm not clear on is why you are attempting to break up fights in a gay bar a few towns out of the way of your home when you're not even supposed to be in town yet."

There is was. The answer to the question he'd been asking himself since he ran away from a situation he wasn't prepared to handle. Bailey had put himself in a few situations, a couple of gay bars and several gut-check moments, to see if he was attracted to men. He'd never gotten a clear answer. Sure, he wasn't disgusted by the men who'd tried to come on to him or the hot looks he'd received, usually from across the bar, but he hadn't wanted to do anything either. His cock had laid dormant in each and every situation. This was going to be a last-ditch effort to find the answer to the question that had circled his mind like a rabid shark and then he was going to put what had happened between him and Scott down in his mind as a wild hair. A little something that had happened when he'd just been dumped by his high school girlfriend, and his emotions were all over the map.

Scott's eyebrow shot up like he didn't want to have to ask the question again, but Bailey didn't know what would come out if he spoke, so he could only shrug in response.

"You don't know why you're here?" Scott continued in a harsh voice, and damn if Bailey's cock didn't chub out a bit more.

Fucking hell. "I don't want to talk about it," Bailey answered quietly after a few deep breaths.

Scott puts his hands up like Bailey had used a safe word, and this conversation was now over. "That's cool, man. I'll be off in an hour or so. We could catch up or I could take you home."

Bailey's eyes opened wide, and Scott worked hard to clarify.

"Wherever that is tonight—I'm guessing either a hotel or Ollie's house."

It would have been easier if the man had propositioned him like he had the last time he'd seen him. Bailey took a step toward Scott, and the man moved backward a bit. Bailey tried again, but the same thing happened. This process repeated itself until Scott was practically against the wall. Bailey was still a good four inches taller than Scott and a good deal heavier, but Scott didn't look like he was intimidated. He didn't look interested either, and damn if that didn't pinch a bit. As a teen, Scott would follow him around physically or just with his stare, and Bailey had enjoyed it, although he mostly acted like he didn't realize what was happening. It made him feel very protective of his friend's little brother. Sometimes Bailey could almost claim the boy was like a brother to him too, but then there were other times he'd find Scott watching him, and it didn't feel familial at all. The boy he knew was a grown man now, and the adoring looks were no longer there. They'd gone from confused surprise after he punched him to curiously wary. Both expressions made him long for the days before he'd killed the flirty smiles and adoring gazes. He knew Scott had changed, but he had too. He was bigger than he'd been when he'd left. The time that had passed made for too many changes. Glancing over at the mirror that was across from them, he took in their reflection. It shocked the hell out of Bailey. He looked like one of the bullies that used to harass little Scott, the way he towered over him. The picture sobered Bailey a bit, and he stepped back.

"Look." Scott took a deep breath and put his hands out in front of him, like he had to deal with annoying and aggressive people like him all the time, and Bailey was just one of the many people he had to battle during any given day. "I'm not sure if you had too much to drink or what, but you've probably been on a plane all day if you came here from Germany. You've got to be tired and discombobulated. Let me get someone to drive you back to you where you need to go."

Bailey took another step backward and was ashamed of what he was doing and even more ashamed of what he was thinking about doing. The reason he'd come to this bar was to find out, once and for all, if he was attracted to men. Up until the moment he'd spotted Scott at the door, the answer was what it had typically been...Meh. Nothing had happened to him like the time he and Scott sat in the back of his truck until it got way too dark to see anything but the stars. It was the last time he'd seen him alone, and now he was rock hard in a bathroom and trying to crowd the man. He stepped back more. "I don't know what came over me. I'm sorry and thanks for getting me a ride, but I can just call a taxi."

Scott let out a breath that sounded a lot like relief, and fuck if the smile that came after it didn't help the situation in his pants ease in the least. What did help was knowing the man that had been in the back of his mind since the last time they'd met wasn't as interested in him now as he had been back then. Bailey didn't know what that meant because he'd planned to have this figured out before he saw Scott again, but it looked like it really didn't matter one way or another.

"I think Mark is out there. He's the owner, and I'm sure I can get him to give you a ride. Come on out when you're ready." Scott kept his eyes on Bailey—not like he'd done in the past and not like he was afraid to turn his back on him. It was almost like he couldn't believe he was there.

The bathroom door closed slowly leaving Bailey standing in the middle of the room. The first meeting with Scott hadn't gone the way he'd thought it would, but Bailey still had questions about himself that had to be answered. Unfortunately, it seemed like they wouldn't be answered by Scott, and he wasn't sure how he felt about that. No. That was a lie. He knew how he felt...disappointed. That was a feeling he knew a lot about, but now that he was starting his civilian life, there were going to be changes. Fewer regrets and more spontaneity was the strategy he was going to use going forward. He'd put some things in motion for himself before he'd come home, like meeting back up with his high school sweetheart who'd just gotten a divorce, but it hadn't felt right. Nothing ever seemed to be comfortable.

It reminded him of the stories his mother would read to him when he was little about the three bears: something was either too hot or too cold, too hard or too soft. Nothing had ever felt just right, but he wasn't going to stop searching until something did.

Chapter 2

SCOTT WALKED OUT OF the bathroom and into the office of the club owner, who was also his best friend, Mark, before plopping down on the loveseat against the wall.

"What the hell is the matter with you?" Mark said after a few minutes of silence. "You look like you've seen a ghost."

"Could you take someone back to their hotel or find him a hotel... whatever, just get him out of your club?" Scott hated the way he was feeling and normally wouldn't ask for help, but there wasn't anything he could do about this without help. His sanity was on the line.

"Is someone causing trouble that you can't handle?" Mark said, getting up like he was off to kick ass. Scott chuckled, and Mark looked over at him. "I've never known you to back down from any fight and if there is someone who's got you in here tapping out, I've got your back."

"It's not like that. You know I don't let anyone get the best of me," Scott said. "If it got that bad, the ambulance would have to pull me out of here."

"That's what I figured, but your vibe is throwing me off."

"Let me process it before I get into it with you. For now, could you take a friend of my brother where he needs to go?"

Mark stared at Scott for a minute and he hoped the man's intuition just shut the fuck up for a few minutes and he didn't ask—

"Tell me it's not the infamous Bailey that I'm taking out of here." Mark's wide eyes and piercing gaze dared him to lie and Scott wanted so badly to say no.

Scott didn't answer, he just sat with what he hoped was a blank look on his face.

"It is him? The man whose name you moan in your sleep. The reason you seem to like bear-like men with dark hair...hell, the reason you saddled up to me when we first met years ago?"

"Yeah, this run down memory lane is great, but I asked a favor and you don't seem to be doing much but having fun at my expense. So get your ass in gear and get him out of here." Scott put his head back on the couch and closed his eyes. His heart was beating harder and faster than it should be for this extended amount of time. It was a good thing he had the ability to keep what he felt off his face because he didn't want Bailey to know how happy he was to see him again, but he didn't want Mark to know that information either.

"Alright, I'll do it for you."

Scott sat there with his eyes closed and knew that this wasn't going to be as easy as he'd hoped because Mark was still in the room and it didn't appear that he was moving in the direction of following his request. Scott took a deep breath, opened his eyes and spotted his buddy leaning against the door. "I guess there is a catch."

"I want you to introduce me to him." The smile on Mark's face indulgent.

"What? You don't need one. Just go out there to the man I describe to you and tell him you'll be taking him back to his hotel." Scott almost couldn't believe what he was hearing, but the look on Mark's face didn't change so he knew that his demand probably hadn't either. "Why?"

Mark looked away from him for a few seconds like he was thinking up a reason. Scott knew that whatever he came up with would have a sprinkle of the truth, but there was going to be a portion of fabrication within his words.

"I just want an introduction."

Scott frowned and stood up. "You're being an asshole, and don't think I don't know what you're doing. I told you, I made a promise to my brother not to mess with his friend again, so this jealous boyfriend act is unnecessary and stupid."

"If you want his departure expedited then that's the only catch." Mark opened the door and waited for Scott to walk out in front of him.

"Fine." Scott stood up and walked past Mark determined to get this damned introduction done and Bailey away from him with those questioning eyes that, if he wasn't mistaken, were filled with interest. All Scott wanted was a simple life. Find a guy who knew he was gay and had made peace with himself and the world about it, set up house, have hot sex and intelligent conversation at the ready any time he wanted. That wasn't too much to ask, was it? He was done with impossible dreams or straight men who wanted to see if they were gay. All he had to do was get through this, the welcome home dinner and then he could concentrate on ignoring the man who was always on the sideline of his mind.

Scott approached Bailey, who was sitting on a bar stool, noting how his stomach knotted up when he tapped him on the shoulder, but that knot had nothing on the release of butterflies that fluttered low in his belly when he turned around and those deep blue eyes found his. He'd just do this like ripping off an adhesive bandage. Quick and painful as hell.

"Hey Bailey, this is Mark, the guy I told you about who owns the place. He's going out and can take you where you need to go. Mark, this is Bailey, my brother Ollie's best friend, in from the military." Scott could feel Mark standing so close to him, he could feel the man's warmth and practically the outline of his cock. *What the fuck was going on?*

Mark moved from his place of possession behind Scott to get closer to Bailey when he stood up. The two men sized each other up and Scott saw a lot of similarities with the build and coloring, but that's where the likeness ended.

"See you at the dinner tomorrow, Bailey." Scott wouldn't run from anything anymore, but he was going to do a fast walk away from this fucked up situation. He was caught by his arm and spun around.

"I didn't expect to see you here, but it was good to see you." Bailey pulled him into a hug and Scott gave him two slaps on the back before he pushed away. Being that close to the man in the bathroom was startling in how intense nostalgia was, but the feeling he had just now wasn't anything like that. It was new, fresh, lust that was as powerful as an explosion. The smell of Bailey was something he'd never forget, but he'd not been in contact with it for so long Scott had told himself he wouldn't be affected like he'd been before, but with that one whiff, his thought process changed. Pushing away from Bailey he took a few steps backing away from the pure temptation that was Bailey.

"See you tomorrow." Scott then turned, walked away from the pair and went back to his post at the door. That man was potent and for the first time he wondered if he'd be able to keep his promise to his big brother.

Chapter 3

WATCHING THE QUICKLY retreating back of Scott the night before was like a splash of cold water, but the smug look on Mark's, the man Scott had foisted him off on, face made him wonder if the two of them had something going on. Either way he was going to back off Scott. He'd see him at the dinner, be cordial and then work on getting his life back together. Find a job, get physical therapy started and start his life as a civilian. He'd taken a taxi back to the airport and stood outside waiting for Ollie to pick him up. The midsized luxury car stopped in front of him like the man thought he'd be late and his very best friend hopped out of the driver seat.

"Fuck, it's good to see you man." Ollie said in his ear since he had the man in a tight squeeze.

"It's good to see you too." Bailey couldn't hold his smile back at the unusual display of affection from his typically laid back friend. He also couldn't believe how much he'd missed Ollie.

"I didn't think you'd ever come back. You haven't returned since you left for basic training, right?" Ollie pushed away from him giving a few slaps on his arm before turning to walk to his trunk, nodding at Bailey's shrug.

Bailey followed along and felt a sadness that he'd stayed away so long and wondered if the emails and the few packages he'd sent hadn't been enough. "Well, I'm back now and I don't think I'll be heading out anywhere soon." Bailey grinned at Ollie and was glad to see the smiling nod from his friend.

"You'd better not." Ollie slammed the truck door closed and went to the driver's seat, sliding in and waiting for Bailey to get situated. "You cut it close. Your mother has called me three times to make sure I'd be here to get you."

"That sounds like her." Bailey looked out the window as they pulled off. He shook his head wondering who all was going to be there.

"She's not that bad. The woman just wants to see you and soon. Nothing wrong with that."

"Nothing at all but I couldn't stand to live at home again. It would be too much, but I promise to visit her a few times a week so she can get tired of me and then we can settle into a more maintainable schedule." Bailey looked over to his friend who was now acting like he was focused on driving. "What's up?"

"Nothing...nothing."

Ollie couldn't lie for shit and Bailey knew something was wrong, but he also knew he'd only get the information when his friend was ready to give it. "Well, I guess I'll find out what nothing is eventually."

"I'm working up to it." Ollie kept his eyes on the road as he worked out whatever he needed to say. Bailey knew he'd hear it eventually and since he'd made his friend wait for his return he could show some patience too.

"Fine." Bailey shook his head and amazed that they could fall into the familiar patterns they'd been in so long ago. "I'll be ready when you are."

They'd fallen into talk of sports and people who remained in the area. Whenever he spoke with Ollie it was like no time had passed. It was as though they just picked up like they'd hung out the day before. Bailey had missed the easy camaraderie and looked forward to spending more time with his best buddy.

They pulled up to his childhood home and Bailey was surprised at how much he'd missed everything. He'd taken off that summer after high school and in the beginning he'd not wanted to come back and confront all the questions Scott had stirred up within him, but later he'd really not had the time. His parents decided that they'd come to him and had visited wherever he was. Mom thought it a fabulous reason to see the world. He'd been a coward before, but the day he woke up in a hospital because he'd run into a burning building to save a mother and small child, he made a few decisions. The fact that he could have died before ever finding out the answers to questions he had about himself, his sexuality and his best friend's brother Scott, had made Bailey grow a bigger set of balls and a new leaf at the same time. He was offered early release because he was going to need a bit of rehab and by the time he'd have been up to par it would be time for his release. Normally, he just rolled the old term into a new term, but not this time. It was time to stop running and start living...whatever that meant he was going to do it.

"Ready, Bailey?" Ollie sat on his side of the car and Bailey looked over at him. Unsure of how long he'd been sitting there staring at the house he could hear the concern in his voice. "You know, no one would blame you if you didn't want a big coming home party. It was just yesterday I learned from your mother that you recently got out of the hospital. Why didn't anyone tell me sooner?"

"I didn't want anyone to make a big deal out of it. I had decided to come home and you know how much I hate pity parties." Bailey stared at the house for a couple reasons, but the main one is he knew his statement would probably not be taken well, because when he really thought about it, his reasoning seemed selfish as hell.

"You're such an asshole," Ollie scoffed. "It would have killed us all if you'd had died."

"I know." Bailey hit Ollie in the stomach with the back of his hand playfully before he opened the car door. "That's why I'm back. I missed this place."

"Well, this place and its inhabitants missed you too, jerk." Ollie got out of the car and walked up beside him elbowing him softly. "That would have been harder, but I don't know the extent of your injuries and I don't want to break you before your party."

"I have an injured shoulder. It popped out of socket when half the roof fell on me, but I'd done what I'd wanted to do by then so all's well that ends well."

"I know about your superpower of understatement, so I'm going to assume you were halfway dead when someone got to you." The concern in Ollie's face made him want to tell his friend that his injury wasn't as bad as it seemed or at least it wasn't that bad now.

"It was over six weeks ago. I'm a little sore sometimes, but all in all I'm back to normal. Feel free to elbow me with full strength next time." Bailey was glad to see the smile back on Ollie's face.

"Don't ever stay away that long again, man. This place has been way too quiet without you."

"I plan on being here until I figure out what to do next." The closer they got to the door the more excited Bailey was to see the occupants of the house. It was like he could feel the warmth and happiness of the people inside.

"Then I plan on finding you some inspiration to stay," Ollie said as he opened the door and walked in.

Bailey knew he should have stopped his buddy in that vein of thought because women loved Ollie and he had no doubt that his friend would bombard him with all types of women to see if anything stuck. It was too late to say anything now as he followed behind Ollie thinking of how to get his friend not to find him inspiration. When the man had gotten his first real girlfriend in high school, he was on a mission to make sure his best friend had one too. Not that Bailey particularly wanted one. He was happy playing volleyball and shooting the shit with his friends, but he'd settled down with Honey. Beth-Ann Honeywell. She was a sweet girl who was the minister's daughter. No one could believe he'd picked her to be his girlfriend including Honey. The loud squeal brought his thoughts from the past back to the present.

"I'm so glad to see you." His sister, Hazel jumped up and wrapped her arms around his neck in affection while giving him a kiss on the cheek. He set her down to the floor, but she kept her hands on his shoulders. "I was told you don't want a big to do like usual, but tough nuggets."

"It's good to see you too, sis."

"Did I hurt you? I'm sorry I didn't think about your arm." Hazel stepped back.

"I'm okay." Bailey hated to see anyone overly worried about him, but he really hated when he upset Hazel.

"You're probably not, but I'm so glad you're here. We have to do something soon."

"Definitely," Bailey told her as she pushed him into the kitchen.

His mother was making a feast for the whole community apparently as it seemed she had made all of his favorite foods at one time. "Mom. When you asked what I wanted when I came home, I said something simple. This doesn't look simple at all."

"Harold, I can do what I think is best when my favorite son comes home." His mother hadn't turned from the stove but was stirring something and replacing lids.

"Mother, I'm your only son." Bailey told her this each time she said called him her favorite son.

"You do like to remind me of that fact, but it's still the truth and I'm sticking to it."

He walked over to stand by the stove and she grabbed his hand. "I could hear your sister shrieking in the other room so I didn't want to do the same thing. I'm trying to hold back."

"I don't like a lot of fuss, but I'm not that bad, Mom. I'm not going to run away because you are happy to see me."

His mother turned and hugged him. *Damn am I so adverse to affection people are afraid to show it to me?*

"We are going to have dinner and then let you get settled at Ollie's place." She held one arm around him and checked pots with the other.

"There's no rush, Mom, I'm glad to be back. What can I do to help?"

"You can get yourself a drink and then talk to everyone who wants to see you." She gave him one more squeeze and then let him go.

THERE GOES MY BAILEY

Bailey pulled a bottle of water from the fridge and could see friends and family gathering outside on the patio while others looked like they were preparing to enjoy the pool. The person he really wanted to see wasn't out there and he wondered if he was going to come. He decided to go to the bathroom before all the 'good to see you and what are you going to do now' talk started.

He walked up the stairs and stopped every few steps to look at the pictures on the wall. They hadn't changed a bit and he noticed how many had cameos of Scott somewhere in the background. When he made it to the bathroom someone was already in there, so he leaned against the wall and waited. He could have gone into his parents' bathroom but it wasn't that urgent. When the door opened, he wished he'd have taken his own suggestion.

Scott walked out and immediately Bailey got hard. *Son of a bitch.* Then he remembered that this wasn't new and that it was a common occurrence when Scott made an appearance. *How had I forgotten that?*

"Welcome back, Bailey. I don't think I said that last night." Scott sounded matter of fact, but Bailey's body only seemed to hear 'last night' and went back to the date he'd had with his favorite fantasy and his right hand.

"Thanks, Scott." Bailey didn't have to think about holding a conversation as the man had walked away after his welcome and Bailey was offering his thanks to the back of Scott's head.

Bailey did his business in the bathroom and washed his hands but couldn't help missing the old Scott. The one who would have waited for his response eagerly with a smile. The one who would have waited the few minutes it took to go to the bathroom to share a few private moments while they walked to the patio. In the stark morning light the situation wasn't much different than it was the dim bar area with a few drinks in his system, the answer was the same. Scott had changed and he was not interested, but that still wasn't going to stop him from getting some answers to some sexually based questions. Thoughts of sliding his cock into a male mouth and videos of frottage shouldn't make you come harder and faster than you could ever attempt to do with thoughts or videos with women in them. Should it? The fact that the mental images all changed to Scott when he was ready to release was something he was going to have to change. He could do that...no problem. With that resolved, he decided to try his best to act normal around the man for the party and then leave that man alone.

* * * *

WITH THE PARTY WINDING down and everyone's bellies full of food and drink, Bailey could say that he'd been hugged and kissed more this day than he'd been in his whole life. He'd lived to tell the tale and was honestly humbled by the warmth and appreciation his very neglected friends and family seemed to have toward him.

"You about ready to go?" Ollie asked, looking more nervous than he had when they were in the car earlier.

"Sure. I'll go say goodbye to my mom and pop. I'll meet you by your car." Bailey walked away but kept his eyes on his friend's face. Whatever it was he wanted to say was tearing him up inside. It probably wasn't anything big and if it had to do with furniture Bailey had more than enough money to help with that. He located his mother sitting in the living room with his aunts and pop. "I'll be over once I get settled and we can talk a bit more."

They all stood up and he had round two of hugs and kisses before he got out of there, plus a bag full of his favorite foods. He walked toward Ollie's car and could see him and Scott having a discussion that didn't look too pleasant, but he was too far away to hear what they were saying. They stopped talking before he could reach either of them and it was silent when he got to the car.

"What's up, fellas?" Bailey tried to lighten a mood that seemed a bit heavy.

"Scott was looking for a roommate because his last one just bailed. Off to train to be a ninja for a show on television and I thought of a perfect solution."

Bailey knew exactly why Scott looked like he did. He was getting a 250lbs man dumped on him. "It looks like only one of you think the solution is perfect. Hey, it's no problem. I can stay at a hotel for a few days until I find something. Worst case scenario, I stay here with my parents. They would love it and I'd not mind too much."

"We both know how much you don't want to do that. I've had an issue come up lately. I've been living with a woman who was having trouble with her ex so she and her daughter have been with me for about a week. She doesn't have anywhere to go and I offered her the same room I offered you." Ollie looked devastated.

"Hey, man. It's not a problem. I know all about your knight in shining armor shit." Bailey reached out and hit Ollie's shoulder playfully. "Let me get my bag out of your car and I'll just stay here."

Ollie and Scott must have followed him to the back of the car because when he got there they were both there just looking at him.

"What?"

"I don't know... you're just kind of accepting of things now. In the past if things didn't go the way you'd planned them you'd get upset and then you'd go quiet. I didn't know how to get around this because I damned sure didn't want you mad at me after you've just returned." Ollie stood in front of him with Scott at his side. Bailey tried not to look at him at all. It pinched a bit that Scott had been arguing about not wanting Bailey to come home with him. He'd figured he was uninterested in him, but he didn't know any type of friendship was off the table.

"I've grown up. Things happen and situations change. I'd rather not get mad about the way life goes. It's easier to just go with it." Bailey turned to the trunk. "Pop this thing for me and I'll get you get going. Oh, and give this to your friend and her daughter. I'm sure she'll appreciate it." He handed the bag of goodies to Ollie.

"Wait a minute," Scott said, stepping in between both of them. "I do have a spot up for rent. I'm trying to decide if I'm staying there or moving somewhere else cheaper. I have to decide if I want to sell it or not, but I don't have a problem with you moving in."

"I just watched you and your brother argue about it so I don't think that's entirely true. I don't want you to do something you don't want to do because you feel bad. I'll stay here with my parents and find a place later. It's not an issue."

Scott turned to his brother. "Give me a few minutes to talk to Bailey alone."

Ollie looked between the two men and then nodded, but he gave a pointed look at Scott. "I have to go to the bathroom before I hit the road anyway."

There was silence as the two men waited while Ollie put his package of food in the back seat and then walked slowly back to the house.

Scott leaned on the trunk of the car and looked at the ground. "Do you not want to move in with me because I know where you were last night and how hard you are trying to keep that a secret?"

"I'm not trying to keep anything secret." Bailey looked away from Scott with that one, but then turned back to watch him recline easily on the car. He didn't remember Scott being so comfortable with himself. It looked good on him and made it hard to look away.

"So coming into town a day early and visiting a bar that's known for engaging men who enjoy sex with other men, sleeping in a hotel and then going back to the airport so his best friend thinks he just got in today sounds like a man trying to keep a secret? I'm not judging you. This was just the rebuttal to your 'I'm not trying to keep anything secret' response." Scott's eyes were clear and so was his thought process.

Bailey wasn't sure what to say about that, so he didn't say anything at all.

"If you moved in with me you could do whatever you wanted, and no one would be the wiser. You appear to be in question mode. It's nice when you have a place to go and explore where you don't have to worry about being judged and or persecuted.

I won't ask any questions and I won't give any advice unless asked." Scott took a deep breath. "How does that sound?"

That whole speech made Bailey want to roar. Not only was Scott not interested, but he had no issue with him experimenting in the same house they'd be sharing. This meant that Scott was also free to bring home 'friends'. Right? He backed up a little from the man who was making him dizzy, because it was difficult to watch him and form rational thoughts that didn't include touching or tasting the man in front of him.

"What are you thinking?" Scott turned to him and waited.

Bailey needed to pull himself together. Beside possibly wounding or killing anyone Scott brought home, it was a good idea. Maybe then he could get to thinking about Scott as just a friend and then he could see what that would mean.

"I'm thinking it's a pretty good idea." Bailey hated that it came out sounding like a military officer's bark, but it was hard to hold whatever had come over him inside.

"Great. I'll get the trunk open and you can get your bag."

"What were you guys doing? Holding my stuff hostage until I listened to reason?" Bailey asked as the trunk opened.

"I'm not sure what my brother was doing, but I just wanted you to think about the benefits of coming with me."

"When I walked up it didn't look like you were listening to reason. You didn't want me to move in with you. Why change your mind?" Bailey dumped his big duffle bag into the back seat of Scott's Jeep.

"I didn't know the reason why Ollie wanted you to stay with me. Listening to that love struck fool made me want to take some of the stress off his plate. You know how he gets about the people he cares about. He was torn and he thought you'd be upset with him. Who knows how long he's been chewing on finding an answer to that problem."

Ollie came jogging down the path from the house and stopped when he got to the car. Looking at both of them, he nodded and a smile spread across his face. "Everything worked out. Huh?"

"Yep. Bailey agreed to stay with me so you don't have to worry about anything." Scott walked over to his brother and patted him on the shoulder.

"Great. I love when things all work out. Now I'll know where to find you and I won't worry that you aren't enjoying your time home. Scott's house is the ultimate bachelor pad and you can bring whoever you want there any time." Ollie wiggled his eyebrows like he did in high school when he was talking about scoring sex with the ladies.

"Right," Scott agreed and then moved to get in the car. "We'd better be going so I can get him settled at the house."

"Okay, then," Ollie gave another hug to Bailey, handed him back the bag of food Bailey had given him that was in his back seat before standing back to watch them prepare to leave.

Inside the car the both of them waved to Ollie and watched as he waved back and then turned around to go back to the house. Probably to get a plate of his own to take home. "When did you tell him about needing a roommate?" Bailey locked his door and put on his seatbelt.

"This afternoon. He lit up like a Christmas tree, but he didn't say anything about his plan until he called me over to his car. I'd just heard the idea."

"And immediately said no."

"That was my first response, but I can see the error, possibly the benefit of both of us in it." Scott pulled off slowly and maneuvered around all the cars on the grass.

"What do you get out of this?" Bailey's heart sped up just a little. Maybe he didn't want to move in with him because it would be too much of a temptation. It's possible the man was just supremely good at hiding his emotions.

"The rent gets paid. Splitting the rent is going to take a lot of pressure off me. I didn't know how I was going to scrape together all the money. I was going to have to start enjoying ramen noodles by the box again or pay more visits to my relatives for food. I don't work a part time gig at The Male Box for the perks. I enjoy my house in the woods, as my brother calls it, but the upkeep and mortgage are a pretty penny."

"Good to know I can be a help to you." Bailey looked out the window and tried to see the good in this. It wasn't happening for him right now, but he was sure something would come to him.

They got to the bottom of the mountain where he supposed Scott lived and the man turned his amber eyes his way. "You can hold on to the 'Oh shit' handle above the window or lay back and enjoy the ride, but either choice comes with a bumpy ride."

Bailey sat up and grabbed onto the handle. "I'm ready for whatever you got."

Scott gave him a smile that went straight to his cock. It was confident and wicked. *What the fuck have I done?*

Chapter 4

WHAT THE FUCK HAVE I done? Scott watched Bailey walk into the house with his big military green duffle bag and knew he shouldn't have said a word while his brother tried to tell Bailey the reason he couldn't come home with him. Scott knew something was going on with his big brother, but they mostly just stayed out of each other's hair when it came to relationships. From the time he'd come on to his big brother's best friend and the man took off to parts unknown for military service, they'd tiptoed around the topic of Bailey. He'd told Ollie what happened between them and he didn't think he'd ever seen his brother so upset. Scott could see his brother's red face and tight posture like he was there now. Ollie had never had a negative thing to say about his brother's sexuality or who he was as a man, but he could tell he was pushing the boundaries when he'd told his brother, whom he'd told everything, what had happened between him and Bailey.

"So you mean to tell me you were in the back of a pickup truck in the dark of night and just crawled on top of Bailey?" Ollie narrowed his eyes and balled up his fists.

"In a nutshell, I guess, but there was a lot more to it and he didn't push me off or yell at me. I'm guessing he liked it." Scott hadn't ever been afraid of his brother and he wasn't going to start now, but he was mentally going over the instructions he'd been given by Bailey about throwing a punch.

Ollie stood in the middle of the room looking like he wanted to bawl or hit something. It was probably both. "He liked it so much he went to stay with relatives until he ships out three weeks from now? I've not seen or spoken to Bailey since a week before you drove him away."

"I don't think I drove him away."

"You did. He's a straight guy, Scott. He stuck up for you in the school and in the streets more than even I have. They would have given him shit about it more if he wasn't as big as he is, but he did all that for you because he's my best friend and this is how you repay him? He cares about you too much to hurt your feelings."

Scott didn't think that was true, but what did he know? He'd just let his hormones run away with him and when he'd straddled Bailey's big body he knew he'd felt the man's hard cock respond against his. He'd moved his mouth down to Bailey's and waited, but it was Bailey's large hand that cupped the back of his head and brought it the rest of the way toward his mouth. It was amazing that they'd not started a fire with the way they'd rubbed their denim covered cocks together, but they'd both come in their pants as they strained against each other. Afterward, they lay together until it got too cold and although Scott tried to hold it back, he shivered. That seemed to break the bond of whatever they were going.

"Excuse me, Scott," Bailey said as he waited for Scott to get off him.

"Oh yes, sure." Scott didn't know what to do or think, but Bailey had hopped down from the cab and gotten in the car. Scott scrambled to follow him. Not a word was exchanged until Bailey pulled up to his house. "We still going to the volleyball game tomorrow?"

"Nah. I think I'm going to pass. Take care of yourself, Scott."

Scott got out of the truck and Bailey zoomed away as soon as the door closed. It wasn't until later that Scott wondered about the way he'd said goodbye. It had sounded so final.

"Which room is mine?" Bailey's deep, rich voice startled him and got him into action.

"Right up the stairs, first door on the left. There is a bathroom between our rooms, but there is one down here as well."

Bailey just nodded and went in the direction he'd been told. Scott wasn't done kicking himself. Had he actually told the man he could experiment with men in this house and he'd not balked at that? He'd seen him in a pick-up bar, but he just couldn't believe that the man was interested in men. There was something that was making him think about it and damn it he refused to be pissed about it. He made a promise to his brother and he would keep it. Besides, he didn't think he could be an experiment for Bailey. He already wanted to keep the man to himself way too much. So if and when Bailey changes his mind and figures out that this was just a phase, he can tell himself he returned the favor from his youth. Helping Bailey the way he'd helped him...not exactly the same way or the same material, but learning was learning.

Scott was still trying to get himself acclimated to the decision he'd made off the cuff when Bailey found him in the living room. He was just aimlessly wandering around his house and must have just stopped here when Bailey found him.

"You settled in already?" Scott said, hoping he sounded like he was making a joke and not slightly freaked out by his sudden appearance. He had on the same clothes, but he looked more relaxed.

"I've got one duffle bag. I threw it on the bed, washed my face and here I am. I didn't have any plans because I thought I'd be up half the night shooting the shit with Ollie."

"You still can. I'm sure if we call him up, he'll be here in a flash." Scott reached for his phone thinking that may be the thing that gets him out of here for a bit.

"That's okay. I got the feeling he was looking forward to going home to fulfill his knighthood. You know how he is when he thinks someone needs his help." Bailey went to the kitchen and Scott could hear him opening up the fridge. "What do you think about us cracking a few of these beers?"

"Sounds good." Scott moved to the single, adjustable chair that he loved so much. It was comfortable and right now he needed to be more comfortable and less stressed. He felt tight and uncomfortable. That isn't what he wanted Bailey to see.

The large man walked into the room and Scott focused on the beer in Bailey's hand.

"You've got good taste in beer," Bailey said, holding one out to him.

Scott took it and had to smile. He'd bought this brand of beer ever since that night on the truck. He'd never drank beer before, but Bailey had been drinking them all night and that's what his kiss tasted like. Scott had started drinking it when he missed Bailey in the beginning and then it just became a habit to buy it.

"You would think so. It was your favorite brand."

"It was, before I left here. This local label had me beer free for years because I couldn't find its equal. I've craved this shit so many times since I've been away." Bailey popped the top and plopped down on the couch. He took a long pull on the bottle and then looked at the container like he'd missed a lover. "Still tastes so damn good I can barely stand it."

"I'm glad I have something you wanted so much." Scott was sorry he'd said that since it made Bailey sober up a bit and he put his beer on the table.

"So what's going on with you Scott? I know you're a police officer. I know you work part time at a club and I know you like to drive like a wild man in your jeep, but what else is there?" Bailey asked and looked at Scott's face.

He cleared his throat, took a swig of his beer and sat up. This is what he'd always wanted as a teen. Bailey's undivided attention, but now he couldn't do what he wanted with it, so it was a tad too late. "That's about all there is about me."

"You never found a partner?" Bailey questioned while studying Scott. "Was the guy who just stiffed you on the rent or Mark, the guy who owns the bar one of your...um...friends?"

Scott froze for a minute at the mention of Mark. What had that asshole said to Bailey? He knew the man was pissed off at Bailey on behalf of his younger self, but he'd have to tell him to let the irrational anger go. "Why would you ask about Mark?"

"I don't know. There was a bit of tension in the air when you introduced us and he wasn't the friendliest on the ride to the hotel. Nothing I can put my finger on but I just wondered if there was something going on between the two of you." Bailey reached for his beer again. He sipped it a few times before just holding it in his hand.

"Mark and I had a thing years ago, but it's way over. We are just friends now." Scott watched Bailey process that and hoped that little snippet would be enough.

"Why'd you break up with him?" Bailey looked at his can like it could tell him what to say next.

"I didn't. He was done with me. It was for the best. Why did you assume I ended it?" Scott shouldn't have been curious. The thread of conversation would have probably been done but nope, Scott had to keep that shit going.

"Well, I just can't imagine anyone leaving you. Especially a guy like Mark. I would think a guy like that wouldn't ever let you get away." Bailey drank down the whole beer after that last statement. Scott wondered if he'd done that because a lie that big had to be chased down with alcohol or was he saying something that was uncomfortable.

"Well, thanks for that, but it's easier for people to leave me than you seem to think."

"Ouch. Was that a direct hit at me? I know we need to talk about it and now seems as good a time as any." Bailey sat up and clapped his hands together like he was getting ready to put in some work.

"That wasn't what I was getting at and I don't want to break out that story until later...or, as a matter of fact, ever. It's old news, water under the bridge, let bygones be bygones."

"*Okay*, I guess you don't want to talk about it." Bailey chuckled uncomfortably as he rolled the can between his hands.

"Nope. So, what are your plans now that you're home?"

"I have a bit of money saved up, but I think I'll get a little kick around job until I figure out what I really want to do, buy a car to get around and find some physical therapy to work my shoulder out. I'm not on the fast track to do much of anything right now."

"Well, I'm actually off from the department for the next two days, so if I can help you with anything let me know." He wasn't used to the conversation between them being so stilted but there were also things he really didn't want to talk about right now. He'd gone from knowing the man was coming, to seeing him in the gay bar where he worked, to thinking he was going to be staying with his brother and out of his hair, to his being a semi-permanent member of his household. He needed a release, a nap and a drink, but not necessarily in that order.

"I don't want to cause you trouble. I'm sure you're going through a lot just having me here."

"Look, I didn't expect to have you as a housemate. That much is true, but I think it's going to work out. I remember what I promised as one of the perks to staying here at the house with me and I go back to The Male Box tomorrow. Maybe you could come with and see what trouble you can get into." Was it possible for words to taste sour? The words he said to Bailey seriously turned his stomach, but that was the reason he chose to come with him and not stay at home, where everyone knew he didn't want to be.

Bailey huffed a bit and followed it with a smile. Scott would have done anything to get one of those when he was younger...as a matter of fact he did. Entertaining Bailey had been one of his favorite pastimes. It was the reason he knew so much about Honey too. When Bailey had acquired a girlfriend junior year that hadn't stopped Scott's heart from desiring the boy he wanted. Often he wondered why Honey never put up a big fuss when he was there and he wondered if she knew he liked her boyfriend as much or more than she did.

"That sounds like a plan, but I thought you said you were off."

"I'm off from my regular job, but I work at The Male Box fairly regularly." Scott watched Bailey process this and found himself feeling like he was back in high school when he watched this man for hours. He wasn't going to turn back into the love struck fool that he was, but it was going to take him repeating that to himself often to make it not happen.

"Do you mind if I take your car to the store? I need a few things so I can get settled." Bailey hopped up and moved away from the table.

Scott was startled that Bailey wanted to get started so quickly, but he shouldn't have been. That was how the man worked. He'd settle on a plan of action and then take steps to get it done as quickly as possible. It was something he'd admired in him when they were younger. "Sure, the keys are in the bowl by the front door."

"You're not going to warn me not to hurt your baby?" Bailey's wide grin made him chuckle.

"If you are referring to me telling my brother that phrase every time he wanted to use my car, please remember that is the man who has wrecked three cars in his life, and one of them was mine. I trust that you are a good driver and I know you're a military man so you should be able to get me a sweet deal on a new one if you fuck this one up." Scott thought things through, always, so he didn't know why he was thinking about getting cozy with his past crush. They are called teen aged crushes for a reason; they're for teenagers and he was way past that. He just needed his cock to get with the program and remember that. There was no need to keep puffing up and getting ready just because Bailey was around. Maybe it was just a habit, but he was going to need regular releases or he was just going to walk around looking like he was a sex fiend.

"Noted." Bailey nodded and walked toward the door.

Scott was up the stairs and in his room with his hard cock in his hand before he could hear the car take off. Being in the constant presence of Harold Bailey was going to take a little while to get used to.

Chapter 5

THE MALE BOX WASN'T the most elegant club that Bailey had ever been in. With its sports paraphernalia on the walls and the almost stadium like feel of the place. Aluminum chairs and tables filled the room. The smell of delicious food that didn't really match the décor made his mouth water. Beef, seafood and rich sauces filled the air and made him ready to eat.

He'd walked in by himself as Scott went in another way. It was like he hadn't wanted to be seen with him, but maybe it was a work thing. It was not as nerve wracking as the first time he walked in and he even recognized a few of the guys who had been there from the last time. Bailey didn't mind being assessed by the men in the room, but it didn't do much for him. He hoped it wasn't just Scott that got him going because he wasn't sure what he'd do if that happened as the man didn't really seem interested.

Bailey took a seat and was able to order from the bartender fairly quickly. The crowd was growing and the eye fucking had begun...at the bar at least. Unfortunately, he had abso-fucking-lutely no interest in any of these men. It was times like this that he wondered if he had a real interest. He'd never been that into women and the reason he'd chosen Honey back in the day was because she was sweet and funny. Most people thought she was a nerd and she probably was, but there was absolutely no pressure and he truly enjoyed being with her.

"Back again?"

Bailey turned around to find Mark standing behind the chair next to him. He stood there so long Bailey wondered if he wanted him to offer a seat, but that would be weird since it was his establishment. "Yeah. I thought I'd hang out here while Scott works."

Mark nodded, but kept glancing toward the door where they both knew Scott stood. Bailey chanced a glance in that direction and saw Scott looking back at the two of them. The look of warning was clearly for Mark but when Bailey looked at Mark he could tell he was juicing Scott's discomfort for all it was worth.

"Is there a reason Scott is looking at us like he doesn't want you talking to me?"

Mark turned his whole body toward Bailey. "I wouldn't know. Why don't you ask him?"

Bailey didn't like being in the middle of something where he was naked and blind. This thing between Mark and Scott definitely made him feel that way. Just thinking of them in the same sentence made Bailey's skin itch with irritation. Glancing again over to Scott, who was so into watching what was going on at the bar, he wasn't doing a good job monitoring the door, he should have just come over. He looked back at Mark. "I think you do know."

With a deep, breathy sigh Mark sat down next to him and signaled for the bartender to come over. "Give me my usual and give my friend here another of what he's drinking. Keep them coming...this guy's drinks are on the house tonight."

Now Bailey really wondered what was up with this guy who seemed to be staring into the mirror. *How vain was this guy?* The man looked for so long Bailey gave up and looked into the mirror as well. What in the world was so fascinating? The man seemed to be comparing himself against Bailey. He could see the man's eyes darting back and forth in the mirror.

"What's your deal, Bailey?" The man said as he concentrated on Bailey's reflection.

He wished he knew, but he didn't. The man in the mirror didn't look like he was trying to be an asshole it appeared as though he was trying to look out for a friend. He couldn't fault Mark for that. Bailey gave the man the only truth he had. "I'm just trying to figure things out."

The bartender bought over their drinks and set them down in front of them.

"You think moving in with a man who has had a lifelong crush on you is going to help you decide if you like cock or not?"

Bailey turned to look at him. He wasn't sure if he was stunned by the language or hurt that the crush he was talking about wasn't lifelong. It had ended because he'd killed it quite effectively. "The crush thing is ancient history. He's not interested in me like that anymore. It's been years since I've even seen or spoken to Scott."

"And you know he's not interested? How?" Mark took another sip of his drink while Bailey thought of how to put this.

"Things are just different now."

"So I don't have to worry about you hurting him again?"

That sentence stopped Bailey from bringing the drink to his lips. It was like he was frozen. He put the drink back down. "I've never hurt Scott."

"You sure about that?"

Bailey thought about the look on Scott's face when he tried to apologize yesterday about the ill-fated night that had changed his life. "I never meant to hurt him, but there may be something I did in the past that may have stung a little." The smug look on Mark's face made him want to smack the back of his head.

Mark nodded and called the bartender back. When the man got there he moved his hand in a big circle around both of their drinks. The man quickly returned with two fresh drinks.

"Well you seem pretty concerned about me hurting a man you broke up with." Bailey watched Mark's face turn a shade or two pinker than it had been before.

"Did he tell you why?" He looked back at the door and Bailey followed suit. Scott was deliberately not looking at them. He may have been away from the man for a while, but he still knew his idiosyncrasies. Scott was uncomfortable and nervous.

"I didn't ask."

"Maybe you should...ask him, that is." Mark drank down his next drink and Bailey felt compelled to do the same. The bartender seemed quicker to refill or refresh the drinks.

"Since you are here right now and you are the horse with the tale, I'd like to hear it from you."

Mark drank down the next drink and then took a deep breath. "Scott is my friend. All while you were away, I looked out for him and he did the same for me. I'm pushing the boundaries of our friendship sitting here shooting the breeze with you, but I wanted to find out a little more about you and I did."

"Well, isn't that grand." Bailey said, wondering if he should have downed that last drink as it was making him a bit snarky.

Bailey felt a hand on his back and he turned around at the same time Mark did. A very pretty man with blond hair and lots of eyeliner had come over to talk to the two of them.

"Look at you two sitting here like my birthday and Christmas bundled in a two for one package. Do I get to unwrap either of you?"

"Thanks, but no." Bailey felt stupid saying it because he knew it was a rhetorical question, but this man did absolutely nothing for him.

Mark chuckled a little and introduced the man. "Bailey, this is one of my best regular customers. If there were rooms to rent Cary Elliot would definitely live here. Isn't that right?"

"I think you should just put that plan in motion. I'd live here for sure, but who's this? I didn't know you had a brother." The man moved himself closer to Mark as they both seemed to assess Bailey.

"I don't." Mark turned to face the man who now was practically perched on his lap. "This is a friend of Scott's. His last name is Bailey, but I don't recall his first name."

Both of the men looked at Bailey like he was going to supply the information they passively asked for, but he wasn't going to give it to them. He didn't like his first name with a passion and he didn't give it out unless he had to. "People just call me Bailey."

The two men talked among themselves for a few minutes and Bailey took the time to study Mark while he engaged in flirtatious banter with Cary.

"You see the resemblance?" Mark asked when the smaller man left.

"Between us?" Bailey didn't know why he was asking that when it was clear that was what he meant, but he wasn't a big drinker and it seemed like these drinks were getting stronger... or maybe they were being refilled more quickly. "We're both big, with dark complexions...blue eyes, dark hair, but you look more like a rough biker."

"And you look more like a rough military guy." Mark laughed a little and Bailey chuckled a bit too.

"Okay, maybe we do look a bit alike." Bailey picked up his drink to find it empty but the bartender was right there and replaced it with another. "I think I've had enough."

"I've been out here pissing Scott off enough. I like you, Bailey." Mark slapped Bailey on the back before he stood up from his stool. "I'm not sure what you've got going on job wise, but you can help with security or help out behind the bar for me if you'd like until you find something better. I appreciate each and every sacrifice you've made being in the military and I'd love to have you here."

"That sounds great. Thank you." Bailey had no idea why he was shocked at the offer of employment, but it could be because it didn't feel like the man particularly liked him. Maybe the man was partial because, like he said, he appreciated military personnel. It was also possible that Bailey couldn't understand why the man liked him because it seemed they were both interested in the same person.

"So you'll be hanging around for a while this time?"

Bailey figured the man knew a bit of his story, but he didn't feel like going into a full blown rehash so he hoped this wasn't what the man expected of him. "I'm fresh out of the service and

I've missed the hell out of this place and the people here, so I think I'll be here for a good while."

Mark nodded as he looked down into his glass as he rattled the ice cubes around. When he looked up at Bailey again, he had a small smile on his face, but Bailey didn't know the man well enough to tell if it was real or not.

Bailey took in the way the man tilted his head back and drank the remaining sip of his drink, before setting it down with a deliberate thunk. Mark leaned over the bar, pulled a card from the under the counter and handed it to him. "Call me tomorrow."

Bailey put the card away and called the bartender over for a water. He was in the middle of guzzling down that clear delicious liquid when he locked eyes with Scott, who he could see in the mirror in front of him but was standing behind him.

"You ready to go?" Scott said, and Bailey started to notice a trend.

There were times he'd see an attractive man and he'd speak to him casually, and there were other times he'd go to bars or other places to meet men. It was all to see if he could replicate the way his body felt right now. Chest tight, cock hardening and filled with anticipation of what's next. It hadn't ever come. It was only when Scott looked at him, stood near him or touched him, he had the swell of desire and the urge for more.

"You're done already?"

"I got Paul to come in." Scott shifted from one foot to the other and Bailey wondered what was going on.

"Sure, I'm ready." He stood up and followed Scott to the car. Bailey hated to be any form of inebriated. It made his steps unsteady and his tongue loose. There'd never been a time he parted with the drinks he'd imbibed previously, but he knew when he woke up the next morning he'd have wished he had. It was the continuous supply of free drinks that had made him forget how much he hated feeling like this.

Scott started the car and pulled out of the parking lot. Bailey stared at the driver and noticed things about the man next to him that he didn't think he'd ever noticed about any guy. Like how he gripped the steering wheel with his large hands, and the way he shifted the gears like he was a race car driver. Maybe he was horny, but the expert way Scott handled both made him substitute his cock for both scenarios. Drunk, with a hard dick, with a man who wasn't interested, was too much for his brain to take in so he just sat in the dark and watched the street lights make a game of peek a boo of Scott's features. The silence in the car was bothersome, so Bailey opened his mouth and even he was shocked by what came out."

"Kiss me, Scott."

Chapter 6

SCOTT WAS GOING TO kill Mark. He didn't know what the fuck the two of them had been over at the bar talking about, but it drove him so batty he'd begged Paul, one of the other security team members, to come in for him tonight. Unfortunately, that meant he was going to have to work the next three nights in a row, but it was worth it. He wasn't going to take Bailey back there ever again. There were other clubs around he could go to. Scott was going to ignore that jealous pang that squeezed his heart and his stomach. The thoughts of what they'd talked about and the images of ways to torture Mark for making him crazy didn't diminish the longing he'd always felt for Bailey. They'd made it to his front door and he knew the plans he had for his immediate future. He was going to get a drink, lock himself in his room and stroke his cock until the images of him and Bailey led to its usual climax. He shut off the car.

"Kiss me, Scott," Bailey said in a low, deep voice from the passenger side of the car. "I think about how it was years ago and I feel like it couldn't have been as good as I remember it being."

Scott wanted to get out of the car, drag him out and show him how hungry he was. Acting like he wasn't interested was difficult but necessary to keep himself in a good head space. There is no way he wanted to tangle with someone who was unsure of what team he wanted to play for. He knew Honey and Bailey had been talking and she was excited for his return.

Scott was no longer the teenager willing to wait for scraps, but it was hard to deny the soft request next to him.

Scott was going to do it, but he needed to jack off first. He was too sexually charged and he didn't want this to get out of hand. For one, Bailey was drunker than he'd ever seen him and he wasn't going to take advantage of that. The way he was feeling, that kiss Bailey had asked for would turn into a full-fledged fuck, and he didn't want the morning guilt. His or Bailey's.

He'd made it into the house, but could hear Bailey behind him. Dropping his keys on the small table by the door, he decided to forget the drink and go straight to the bedroom. "I'll be right back." Scott threw the words over his shoulder as he escaped the room. A large hand caught his arm and stopped his flight.

"If you don't want to, I understand. You don't have to run from me."

Scott wondered if Bailey saw the fear in his face. His tone said he was trying to comfort him, but little did the man know he was trying to save them both...from embarrassment, guilt and well he was just trying hard not to revert to the love sick fool he'd always been around Bailey. "I'm not running."

"I've run enough from you in the past to know what running looks like. I knew you were going to bolt as soon as the question left my mouth. I'm sorry that I ask—"

That was all Scott was able to take. He was smaller than Bailey but since larger men were his favorite, he knew how to work around that. Pushing the larger man so that he fell back to sit on the couch he straddled him. They were face to face and breathing hard. He wanted so many things from this man, but decided he'd just give him what he asked for.

Placing his hand on the back of Bailey's head, he brought him in as he lay a soft easy kiss on his lips. He could do that and leave. That would fulfill the request and get him out of this mess, but he hadn't anticipated the low moan that sounded like a wounded animal and the way that sound would wrap its way around his cock like an audible, pleasurable squeeze.

Scott could feel Bailey's large hand on his ass as the kiss heated up. Bailey had asked for the kiss, but now that it had been granted, he realized he was just asking for permission because the man fully took charge of everything. Scott wanted it to be a sweet taste, but it was anything but sweet. He rocked his hips to allow his denim covered cock just a slight bit of friction and was rewarded with another groan. He was flipped into a horizontal position on his back with a wall of Bailey on top of him.

"Say you want me."

Scott could feel the responding hardness of Bailey against him and he wanted to have all of their clothes magically disappear. Bailey moved his kiss from his mouth, tracing a pattern to his neck and licking and biting like he was enjoying Scott's flavor.

"Say it," Bailey demanded, but Scott just didn't want to admit anything. Bailey sat up, looked down at Scott as he remained lying on the couch and put his hand over Scott's cock.

It was like he was looking for his body to say what his mouth wouldn't. His cock throbbed against Bailey's hand and Scott was almost embarrassed at how his cock seemed to throb as he thrust against his brother's best friend.

"Looks like I found some part of you that doesn't mind showing how it feels." Bailey seemed fascinated as he rubbed the palm of his hand up and down the length of his boner.

Scott was out of his mind with desire and it was hard to remember why he didn't want this in the first place. The guy of his fantasies was right in front of him. He placed his hand on top of Bailey's and made that light and maddening touch a bit rougher.

Bailey stopped to unbutton the top few buttons on Scott's pants, but Scott moved his hand and pulled him down on top of him. He wasn't ready for any of this, but if he didn't come, his little head was going to continue exerting more power and control over the head that supposedly held the thinking brain. He was done holding back.

Scott licked his tongue over Bailey's prickly stubble and practically attacked his mouth. He wanted to savor this moment. The taste of scotch and mint on Bailey's tongue and the way his breath hitched higher with every thrust of their covered cocks against each other. They were both close and their movements were frantic.

Scott broke the kiss to get the answer to one of his most thought about questions. What does Bailey look like when he comes? "Tell me you've missed me."

Bailey opened his eyes and the look of lust and desire brought Scott that much closer to going over the edge. "I've missed you, Scott."

The words did more than Scott would have wanted and his eyes closed with the force of the orgasm that worked through his body. In the distance he could hear Bailey saying his name over and over as he shook and ground his throbbing cock against him.

The sounds of harsh breaths and the smell of his release filled the room. Scott had missed the answer to the question that always filled his mind and he was silently kicking himself. Bailey's big body was draped over him like a thick blanket and Scott wanted nothing more than to stay under him.

"Let me up and I'll get some towels and stuff so you can take a shower."

Bailey stood up and offered a hand to Scott which he debated on taking. He couldn't even look Bailey in the face and wasn't sure he wanted to know what touching him would do but it would seem hostile. He grabbed hold of the offered hand and was pulled into Bailey's arms. Fuck.

"You're not okay with what just happened, huh?" Bailey asked with the deep sexy voice so close to his ear Scott shivered with fresh anticipation.

"It's cool." He pushed away from Bailey to walk to the door. Scott turned back to look at Bailey and watched his face turn green.

Bailey made a dash to the half bathroom by the front door and Scott could hear the soundtrack of drunkenness. Why had he let all that happen when he knew Bailey was too drunk? He'd done all that and still hadn't witnessed what the man looked like when he came. He walked to get a small trash can and put in a fresh plastic garbage bag, two bottles of water, some ibuprofen, towels and wash clothes before checking on his guest.

He'd made it back to the couch and was laying there with his arm over his eyes.

"I brought this out for you." Scott lay all the items on the table in front of him, put the basket by Bailey's head on the couch and put the cold cloth on his forehead after he moved his arm.

Bailey opened one eye. "You must have sick house guests often."

"It's not typical, but I do know what I'd like when this happens. Drink one water now and take the pills with the other bottle when you wake up." Scott stood up.

"I hate to ask this, but can you just sit here for a minute? I won't ask anything else of you and I won't even talk."

"Sure." He didn't really want to see this giant man be vulnerable because it was doing such stupid things to his head and heart but he couldn't turn down a plea like that either. Scott sat on the couch and Bailey's head was right by his thigh. He wasn't sure how long he was supposed to sit there, but he wished he'd cleaned up while he was running around for supplies. Dried cum wasn't comfortable at all.

Bailey lifted his head and placed it on Scott's lap. His cock trying to fill while trapped in underwear, full of drying spunk was even more uncomfortable, but Bailey... his Bailey looked comfortable and on his way to sleep. Scott took a deep breath, put his head back to rest on the couch and closed his eyes. He'd wait for just a few minutes and then he'd get cleaned off and go to bed.

• • • •

THE BANGING ON THE door woke him and Scott opened his eyes. There was a pain in his neck, it was too bright in the room and the banging wouldn't go away. He looked down and Bailey was fast asleep on his lap still.

"Hey, get up. I have to get the door." Scott helped him lift a bit before trying to get his balance and hurrying to the door. There must be some kind of emergency the way someone was knocking. He pulled open the door. "Honey?"

"My goodness you must sleep like Bailey." Honey always looked like she just stepped off the runway. You'd never know she was a mousy little thing in high school. No one could believe the most sought after boy had picked her over all the other hotter and easier girls in the school.

"Hey, Honey. I was going to ask what brings you here, but I think I figured it out." Scott invited her in and tried not to seethe. This is what he was up against. The whole gay trial he knew Bailey was going through. He didn't doubt Bailey wanted to try some new things and he didn't think it was bad, but it was horrible if he wanted to use Scott. He wanted so much more and he knew he wasn't going to get it. Before he gave in to sleep, he was thinking about just going along for the ride with Bailey because... well because he was Bailey and why not, but first thing in the morning the Universe has shown him why not. Honey.

It was impossible to get mad at the woman though. First of all, she was a good friend and she gave the best hugs. She squeezed hard, she was fully invested and made a noise like she was giving it her all. They'd become friends when she and Bailey were a couple and their friendship had continued after they'd broken up and he'd moved away.

"How was your trip?"

THERE GOES MY BAILEY 55

She whirled on him with a bright smile that made him smile too, even through all his confusion. "It was amazing. I got to see Ireland, Scotland and England. Each and every day I woke up not really sure where I was, but I knew I was divorced from the dickhead I married and my location was gorgeous."

"I'm so glad you had a good time." Scott smiled at how happy his friend was and how much better her color looked from before her trip.

She hugged Scott like usual and he shook his head. His mostly quiet and very routine life had spiraled out of control. He was standing in his hallway, hugging Honey with a dried uncomfortable load in his pants and the man of his dreams on his couch. He couldn't blame it all on Ollie, but for the most part he did.

"Thanks, Scott." She looped her arm in his and they walked down the hall to where he'd left Bailey. When they got to the living room it was empty. "I'm a free woman."

Scott's stomach dropped and he mentally slapped himself and told himself to pull it together. "Is that what brings you here this morning?"

She dropped his arm and turned to him. "I talked to Ollie yesterday and he told me Bailey was staying here with you. I thought he might like to catch up and we can go look for cars. I was with him when he bought his first one and thought it would be fun to look again."

Scott's smile stayed in place. He knew it did because he could feel how tight it was. He called out for Bailey, who was just on his way down the stairs.

"Sorry, I just jumped in the shower really quick. Hey, Honey, how are you?" Bailey made his way down the stairs and gave

Honey a hug. Scott moved away from the couple as they broke apart and started acting like they were long lost lovers...which of course they were.

He'd gotten all the way to the steps when he heard his name.

"Scott, come with us. We'll get something to eat and catch up." Honey's smile was infectious, but he must have had the antidote because he didn't feel like getting in the middle of anything with those two and he definitely didn't feel like smiling.

"No. You two have fun. I'm going to get cleaned up and run a few errands."

Scott's voice carried as he moved away from the reuniting couple and he was nearly halfway up the stairs by the time he finished refusing. He couldn't look back at them because he couldn't stomach how closely they stood together. It hurt too much to see.

"We can stop to do those too." Bailey was at the bottom of the staircase looking up at him. Scott could see that he wanted him to go, but he just couldn't do it. He'd spent his entire life tagging on with others, mostly to get the attention of this very man, but he was done with it.

"No thanks. It's been a full couple of days it will be good for me to be by myself. Have a good time guys." Scott made it to the top of the stairs and into his room before he heard anything else. It was difficult to tell the man no but he was getting better.

He picked out his clothing and went to the shower. On his way out of his room, he saw the happy couple on the way to her car. She was animated and he was listening with a smile on his face as he watched her antics and Scott sat in the shadows. It was just like old times.

Chapter 7

Bailey sat at the local diner after consuming what had to be his weight in food and watched Honey. She had a way of telling a story that pulled everyone in and made them invest in the tale, but he couldn't keep his thoughts away from what had happened this morning. He had heard Honey's voice at the door and had made it up the stairs and into the shower in record time. He was happy that he'd woken up earlier taken the medication and water Scott had brought for him and went to the bathroom. The man was still asleep on the couch and although he should have woken Scott up so he could get some rest he found he didn't really want to. Bailey had gotten sick looking at the expression of self-incrimination on Scott's face. He didn't have the words to explain that he was enjoying all they'd done on the couch and then the alcoholic drinks he'd consumed decided come back to have a second showing of themselves.

"I just can't believe you're back."

Honey had gone through the story she was on and he'd missed it. The look on Scott's face haunted him. He'd hoped they'd be able to talk this morning. Clear up some things and maybe move on to...hell if he knew he was still trying to figure his shit out, but what he did know is he wanted more time with Scott.

"Here I am."

"I know you need physical therapy and I know you need a car. I can help with both." She smiled, and he wondered if she was really this happy or was something going on with her.

"Well, I appreciate all the help and the smiles that accompany them, but I've got to ask. Why are you so hell bent on fixing all my problems today?" Bailey poured a bit of cream into his coffee.

"I've always felt bad about how you left. We never really talked about it. Even when I decided to be your pen pal while you were away you never asked for an explanation or anything. I wanted to believe you left because of me, but you never fought for me so I'm not sure."

"You dumped me so I would chase after you?" Bailey stopped stirring his coffee and looked at her. "Surely you're not that callous."

"Of course not. There were some things that were missing from our relationship when we were younger and I was mad that you didn't seem to have any passion for me." Honey's bright smile was gone, and a bit of vulnerability remained.

"Honey, I loved you with everything I had. I didn't know how to do anything different, but I'd have done anything you asked. You turned to me one day and told me you were done. We hadn't fought, you didn't accuse me of anything, it was just the end. I tried to talk to you twice and you had first, your friends, and then your father, tell me to leave you alone."

Honey looked away and Bailey hoped to hell she didn't cry. It broke his heart, even if he hadn't done anything wrong.

"I knew you loved me, Bailey, but you weren't *in* love with me. I wanted more than that and I wanted more for you." She returned her gaze to him and although it was bright and shining it looked like she'd kept the tears at bay.

"I have no idea what you're talking about now or what you wanted from me then." Bailey waited for more because she seemed to be speaking in riddles.

"You had eyes for someone else back then and it drove me crazy," Honey said softly.

"What?" The frown on Bailey's face was so quick and hard it hurt. "Never. I was never unfaithful to you and I didn't have anything for anyone but you. I was with you all the time unless I was with Ollie."

She shook her head. "I'm not going to get into it right now. I stand by what I said, and I feel like I was right, but of all the things we were friends first. I was devastated when you went away."

Bailey shook his head. He didn't understand women most of the time, but he understood Honey the least. "You're saying you were devastated when I went away, but you pushed me away and made sure I stayed gone. Do you see how this doesn't make any sense to me? I spent a good long time wondering what I did that made you treat me as if I'd done something to you, but I couldn't ever figure it out."

She nodded. "I would do it differently if I'd have known how. I was angry and upset. I was afraid if I told you what my problem was you'd just blow it off. It felt too real to me to hear you deny it."

"So without confirmation that you were correct or that I was with someone you just dumped me and then became sad that I left?"

"It sounds so stupid when you tell it from your side, but I know how I felt then. Although I regret the end result, I stand by my decision to let you go."

"Well, maybe one day you can tell me why and then we'll both know."

"Can we revisit this another day? I'm just so happy that you're back and I'd like to just catch up. You're not planning on moving away any time soon right?" Honey's smile was back even if it was a bit dim, he was happy to see it.

"I'll be right here."

"Good. Let's get out of here and find you a car. Then we can set up a time for me to stretch you out." Honey scooted her way out of the booth and picked up the check.

"Give me that." He snatched the bill out of her hand.

She blew out a breath. "You could never stand when I paid for anything. I woke you up and brought you here so I should pay."

"Maybe next time."

"You always say that," she said as she followed him to the checkout line.

"Because then there's always hope."

* * * *

STANDING BEHIND THE bar of The Male Box Bailey was ready for his first day of work. Not that he'd ever been a bartender, but he had an app on his phone and the other bartender had given him some tricks to getting a good head of foam on a beer so that its picture perfect and there was still a good amount of beer in the glass. He thought he was busy in the military, but today was one for the record books. He was tired. Not physically exhausting, but emotionally he was all over the place. He'd spent most of the day with Honey but he'd texted Scott several times with no response. Found the sweetest ride in the form of an all-wheel drive, four-door flatbed truck and got a call from Mark that they needed him to work tonight.

Bailey had gone back to the house and hoped Scott was there, but he wasn't and he wasn't answering his phone either. He wasn't sure if his new roommate was pissed about anything or if he just didn't feel like being bothered. Showing up at his buddy's job didn't seem like the appropriate thing to do, but he was thankful that he'd been called in to work that day. Bailey wasn't sure what time Scott worked tonight, but he'd make sure they talked about what had happened the next time they were together. Just casually bring up what had gone on between them and the abrupt halt with the arrival of Honey. That's what he'd thought until Scott had shown up at work. There was a smile on Scott's face as he talked to Mark before he glanced over and saw Bailey. Scott returned his gaze to Mark like he didn't feel the same flash of scorching heat Bailey did when Scott looked at him. Mark had his hand on the back of Scott's neck as they turned and walked toward the bar and damn if that didn't piss him off. It shouldn't for a couple of reasons. One, Scott wasn't his and two, the man didn't seem particularly happy to see him. This was going to be harder than he thought.

"You gave him a job?" Scott said to Mark when they got to the bar. The look on his face was incredulous.

"Yeah. He's a military vet and one of your very best friends. Why wouldn't I want to help him out." Mark smiled at Bailey. "Hey, get me a black label scotch on the rocks."

"Sure thing." Bailey tried not to focus on the amount of anger that was rolling off Scott, but it was difficult.

"Scott, can I talk to you for a minute?" Bailey put the drink Mark had asked for on the bar and stood waiting for an answer.

THERE GOES MY BAILEY 63

Scott's eyebrows shot up immediately and Bailey thought he was going to say no but he didn't. He waved him to a place away from the bar.

Bailey didn't even know what to say when he got to the place Scott stopped. "I tried to call you all day today to tell you I'd be here and that I got a car. You're pissed at me is the vibe I'm picking up and I'm not sure why."

"Look, I don't know why either. I'm acting like an ass. I'm glad you've got a job and your own wheels. Now you can find whatever it is you're looking for."

"What? I thought you were mad at yourself because we'd fooled around a little and I was drunk. You don't..."

"No." Scott took a breath like he was going to try to describe what was going on. "Well, yes, I was upset that all that happened when you weren't fully functioning, but I'm not the experiment gay boy for you."

"Who said you were that?"

"This isn't my first time around this track and after the last one, I'm done. I can spot men like you a mile away. You want to know more about being with a guy, you want to know if you really like guys or if it's just the thought that turns you on. I'm comfortable, available and you know I've had a crush on you since puberty hit and I knew what dicks were for."

"I'm sorry that's how it was for you. That was never my plan." Bailey put his hand on Scott's arm and squeezed.

"So...what? Now you're a gay man?"

Scott was getting angry and Bailey didn't know what to do to stop what looked to be an angry barrage of words coming his way. He went with his first thought and brought his lips down on Scott's. He hoped to convey all the things he wanted to say.

He wanted this kiss to prove to Scott that he wasn't playing around, that he wanted to see what was going on between them and he enjoyed kissing him and touching his body. When he could feel Scott's body relax, Bailey took the kiss from reassurance to a deep promise of something dirty. He used his tongue to lick Scott's lips before he sucked one, then the other into his mouth. He wanted to taste the full plate of Scott that was being offered up to him and he didn't want to stop. The man had relaxed a bit more and he wished they'd had more time before they both had to work.

Bailey pulled away from Scott and loved the dreamy look that covered Scott's face. He gave the swollen lips one more quick kiss.

"I'm not sure what's going on with me, but I do know I want to find out and I'd like to find out with you. Nothing in life is promised so I'm not saying I know what will happen, but I've spent a good deal of time wondering about that first kiss I got from you. It was even better than any other I had before or since that night. I also wonder why it's you I think of while I stroke my cock, and why just thinking of you makes me come harder than any pussy I've ever been inside."

Scott didn't do anything but listen and Bailey was encouraged that was a positive sign.

"I'd like to talk about this later, but if it's something you don't want, let me know and I promise I'll try not to look at you the way I really want. I'll try to keep my feelings to myself. We were friends for a long time before that night in the back of the truck. We talked about so many things. Some of them were important and others... not so much, but I want to stop walking on egg shells around you and I want you to do the same. No matter what you decide to allow between us."

Bailey wondered if Scott was going to say anything, because he appeared frozen but then he nodded.

"So we'll talk later?" Bailey said.

Scott looked as if he was just waking up from sleep. "Sure."

Bailey walked away feeling like he was on cloud nine...at least for right now. A glance behind him showed him that Scott hadn't moved. He just stood there right where Bailey had left him. To his left, he saw Mark and the expression on his face. It wasn't happy or mad, but mildly neutral. His balled up fist told another story. It made Bailey wonder again what kind of feelings his boss had for Scott. He'd never once been jealous of anyone or any thing so these feelings that came and went were novel and not particularly pleasant.

He took one last look at Scott, who was now in a stare down with Mark. Bailey's mood went from content to annoyed.

This jealousy shit is for the birds.

Chapter 8

SCOTT WANTED TO BOTH fuck someone up and fuck someone hard. Two very different things with two very different people, but person number one was in his sights. He walked past Mark and into his office. "Follow me."

The door slammed a few minutes later when Mark followed him into the office. "Yes, your highness?"

"This isn't the time to be cute. What the fuck are you doing?" Scott wanted to be his calm self and just take a seat on the couch and work this out, but he was so fucking pissed off, confused, excited and too many other things to think about. The many emotions swirling inside of him weren't mixing well and that concoction just added up to rage. He stood in the middle of the room because he was too hyped up to sit down.

Mark moved to sit behind his desk. "I'm not sure what you mean."

"You're not sure what I mean? Sitting with Bailey and filling his head with who knows what, offering him a job? I live with the man so now my jobs are the only break I get from him and you're screwing that up too."

"You don't want to be with Bailey? The lost love of your life? Why? What's the matter?" Mark was typically a smart ass, but there was something different about this sarcasm and snarkiness. Scott took a few seconds to put what he was feeling on the back burner and try to take a walk in Mark's shoes.

"Are you jealous of Bailey?" Scott was surprised and confused by the expression on his friend's face, but Mark remained silent even after a few moments of waiting. "You dumped me a long time ago and you've never made a move to get that part of our relationship back. Now that you think there is a competition I'm interesting again? I'm not a prize to be won. You're making all these moves and for what?"

"I didn't dump you. I just told you what I thought about why you wanted me and you got mad. You showed me the picture of the man of your dreams, and no you didn't call him that, but you sounded like a teenaged girl every time you talked about him. He looked a lot like me. That night you moaned his name in your sleep and then I knew that you were just with me as a substitute for him."

"What? Fuck you, Mark." Scott couldn't believe the words coming out of his friend's mouth. "How did you hold on to this for so long?"

"I hoped one day you'd stop talking about him like he was the only man for you. Time passed and you never did and then one day he showed up." Mark leaned back in his chair and seemed to take Scott in. It was like he'd been holding all this information in until right now, but there was only so much Scott could take. It was like he was on overload.

"And that meant you were going to force feed him to me everywhere I go because in your mind, I'd chosen him over you?"

Mark sat up in his chair and with the look he had on his face Scott didn't think he'd say another word, but he surprised him. "In your mind, I didn't have a chance. You liked that I reminded you of someone else, but I didn't. I'll admit I thought about you seeing Bailey as an adult and getting a chance to view him without the teenaged adulation, but from what I just witnessed that obsessed teen still resides inside you and still has a thing for Bailey."

Scott's head throbbed thinking about all the things going on in his life and all the fucking weirdness. It was like he had fallen down a rabbit hole and was in his own especially fucked up wonderland. Mark, who was regularly a low maintenance 'go with the flow' type guy was now a jealous manipulator who was trying to make him see Bailey in a negative light, and Bailey the straight man who'd been his protector and brother's best friend was coming on to him, kissing him and being the man he'd always dreamed about. It was enough to give him a migraine. The noise and lights of the club were killing him. Scott knew he'd been running full throttle on fumes for the last few weeks, but the past few days he'd added more stress to his life. He should have known this would happen now with his stress levels on full tilt. Scott stood up and was a bit dizzy.

"I don't feel so well. I'm going to go outside to see if I feel better. If not, I'm going home." Scott didn't even look at Mark as he spoke. He felt betrayed for some reason. Maybe Mark had a reason to be an asshole, but he just didn't have any fucks to spare at this particular moment. He got to the parking lot and stood by his car for a few moments.

The door opened again and he heard the loud noise of the bar get louder and then simmer down as the door closed. He didn't have enough energy to talk to Mark again, but he'd find enough to throw a punch at that fucker if he had anything but an apology coming out of his mouth.

"Hey. Mark said you weren't feeling well and I could take off and get you home." The deep voice reminded him of his teenaged years and almost every jack off session since. Bailey.

"Will you have to come back?" Scott asked. The anger and desire to fuck someone up instantly changed to pure desire to fuck. That wasn't good either.

"Not until tomorrow."

"I don't want to stop your first day of work. I'll be okay. Maybe if I sit in the car for a while I'll be better."

"I'm taking you home now so there is no need to try to talk me out of it." Bailey ushered Scott into the passenger seat and buckled his seat belt. That shouldn't be sexy at all but his head wasn't throbbing as it was before and the scent of Bailey was as comforting as a soft well used blanket.

Bailey climbed into the driver seat and adjusted it to his liking. He was such a big guy it was a wonder he fit in the car, but he made it work. He drove and hummed a tune Scott thought he knew, the road was a bit rocky, but that was probably because the migraines always fucked with his sensory perception. Trying to relax, he took a deep breath of fresh air but ended up with Bailey's scent filling him up.

With all the medications he'd tried and all the remedies he'd researched it was funny that being with this man and breathing him in would be the thing that would bring about some relief. The deep tone of Bailey's voice shouldn't be this pleasant. Should it? It was something Scott wanted to put some thought into but before he couldn't figure it out.

"We're home."

Scott sat up. He must have fallen asleep and if he slept through them getting up the mountain he must have been knocked out.

"I was probably just tired." Scott stretched long and hard. He'd not gotten a lot of sleep the night before. Sitting up in an odd position all night had made his body achy. "Sorry you couldn't stay your shift. New bartenders usually kill in tips."

"Really? I'll have to have my piggy bank with me next time I go to work."

Scott opened the door and liked the thought that they were home. He wouldn't trick himself into thinking this was a long term thing, but it was wonderful for now.

He walked through the kitchen and flipped on the light. "I'm just going to get something to drink and then—" Scott picked out a water bottle and then stopped. Bailey was standing right next to him. He plucked the bottle out of his hands, opened it, took a sip and then handed it back.

"Are you my official taster?"

"I'd like to be." Bailey backed up to the door like he was giving Scott some space. "I've lived most of my life watching it go by and not saying much about how I'm feeling but I'm at a place in my life where I'm going to make some changes."

"Okay?" Scott tipped the water bottle to his mouth and drank like he was a heartbeat away from dehydration.

"Did you hook up with Mark because you think he looks like me?"

Scott choked on the water he'd just been drinking. It took a few seconds before the coughing fits stopped and he could get his thoughts together to form a response. "I knew he was saying something to you about that the other day. That fucker."

"Is that a yes?" Bailey's big blue eyes looked even bigger as he was holding them so wide open.

"That's what he said. Look, I was much younger when I met him. You'd just left and I was at the mall. I swore I saw you and I followed until the man went into the bathroom. I turned the corner and he had me up against the wall asking why I was following him and who was I. Honestly, I didn't care that he was so upset. I was more disturbed that it wasn't you." Scott sipped his water again. He hated thinking back to that time in his life because he was so depressed and sad that Bailey had left.

"Hey. I'm sorry I left without talking to you." Bailey sat down at the table and stole his water bottle again he took another sip.

"Why do you keep doing that? There's more in the fridge." Scott stole the bottle back.

"I just want to taste you. I told you I'd let you have your space and I'd let you think about it, but when I'm around you I want to get as close as I can and stay there. I'm going to grab a water and watch a bit of television so I can keep up my side of the bargain. I can wait for you to work out what you need to." Bailey did what he said he would and walked out of the kitchen.

Scott was torn. Should he just keep things the way they were, tell Bailey to look for another place to stay and keep looking for housemates...ones that didn't make him want to crawl all over them and lick them like ice cream cones. Or should he take a chance, one he's always wanted to take?

Getting up from the table, he finished his water and threw the bottle away. The quandary didn't seem to be getting any easier to figure out. Maybe he'd think better with a shower. If he didn't come up with an answer under the water, then maybe it would come to him tomorrow. He had to work in the morning and a day being one of Langleyville's finest was enough to make him think he should just get some shut eye and put the lid on today.

He didn't want to rush his answer, but it was clear that this inner conversation had lots of different opinions. His head, his cock and his heart all had different agendas that needed to be addressed, but he just didn't have it in him to do it tonight. *Tomorrow is another day.*

Chapter 9

BAILEY HEARD SCOTT leave the kitchen and walk up to his room. As much as it bothered him, maybe he'd have to give up his pursuit of what he wanted with Scott for now. It wasn't like he didn't understand why Scott may not want to take a chance on what Bailey wanted. He knew he wasn't straight, and he understood why this seemed out of the blue to Scott. The man just didn't know it wasn't the first time he'd thought about his sexuality and wondered about his straightness or lack thereof. He'd gone out of his way to look at other men before, but he didn't really feel anything for any other man. He was actually beginning to believe it a fluke? It wasn't until he'd seen Scott again and the zing, that he'd remembered from before he left, ran through his veins like warm brandy. Maybe he should just focus on himself and get his life together. This issue had taken up too much space in his life. He sat up and thought about calling it a night.

"What are you watching?" Scott walked in the room, fresh from a shower and Bailey had his answer. He wanted Scott. All the other questions weren't really important because this dark haired, amber eyed, scruffy faced guy was the damn answer.

"Some kind of crime show. My thoughts were too loud to hear any of what's going on. Did you want to see something else?" Bailey held out the television remote.

He took it out of Bailey's hands and changed the channel to a sci-fi one, then moved to sit next to him on the couch. Bailey wasn't sure what to think about the whole thing so he just watched the television. His heart rate sped up and he could feel the throb of his heart beat in his cock. If he thought the ideas that were in his mind before were loud they were practically screaming now.

"Remember when I didn't want to talk about what happened before you left?" Scott's tone was quiet and it reminded Bailey of how they spoke to each other the night when it all went down.

"Yes, I remember. You said you never wanted to talk about it and that it was old news, water under the bridge, and we should let bygones be bygones. Right?" Bailey asked, knowing he was being a dick, but hoping it would get them back to the friendly camaraderie they'd had growing up. Everything between them was so intense all the time.

"Right," Scott said and then laughed. "Maybe I want to hear about it more than I let on. Now that I think about it."

"Since you had more of an idea of what you were doing, I'd like to hear from you first." Bailey put his hand on the back of the couch and turned toward Scott. Not to intimidate him, but to listen and really hear what the man was trying to say.

The sigh that followed was long and deep…like he'd held that breath since the day Bailey left as a plug to keep in what had happened. "Honey had broken up with you and you were so upset. I'd always followed you around so I was practically there when you were dumped."

"You were very helpful at that time. Ollie had his own girlfriend and although he was comforting it was great having you around."

"You needed me and I soaked that shit in like a thirsty sponge sucks up water. I knew you were going away to the Air Force in a short while, but until that day in the truck it didn't seem real. I appreciated how you and my brother had always kept the bullies away when I was younger, but you didn't know how I really thought of you. I knew you were straight and I also knew you were my brother's best friend, but as we talked about everything and nothing under the stars I felt like you'd understand what I was feeling and maybe you felt something for me too."

The look on Scott's face and his whole demeanor transported his whole tough cop/bouncer persona to the young teen who used to look at him like he could fix the world. He couldn't count the times Ollie wanted the little guy to leave them alone, but Bailey had always welcomed him. He'd liked him being around, but there was more to it, even if he hadn't voiced it to anyone. The day he'd gone over to the house for Scott's birthday party / get together by the pool and the newly 18 year old Scott had hopped out of the pool when he'd arrived had made Bailey feel like he was in the middle of a corny teenage rom-com. He couldn't see anybody but Scott. The workouts he'd been doing were paying off and the lean muscles had grabbed his attention unlike anything else had up to that point.

"Anyway. I put my hand in yours and you didn't do anything, so I straddled your big body like a bronco." Scott glanced at the television, but Bailey could see the small smile on his face, but he wasn't sure if embarrassment or some other emotion made him want a break from eye contact.

Bailey huffed out a laugh thinking about what had happened. "I was shocked, but I also wanted to see what you'd do."

Scott moved a little closer to him on the couch. "I was hard when I hopped on you, but when I felt your thick cock throb under me, I went crazy. I kissed you and rubbed against you like a cat in heat."

"I think we both know there was more to it than that. You want to take the heat for this, but I'm calling foul. You brought your mouth within inches of mine, but you stopped and it was the longest few seconds of my life. I thought it was a pause, but as the seconds ticked away I knew what you were giving me."

Scott looked away from Bailey to the television again and the sight of the man's neck almost did him in. What was it with him wanting to taste Scott's skin? Bailey reached for the remote and turned the television off. Scott waited a few breaths before turning his attention back to Bailey, who was unable to hold his words until his friends amber gaze settled back on him.

"You gave me a chance to stop you. A chance to say no, but I didn't take it, did I?" Bailey put his hand on Scott's face and turned it toward him. "Did I?"

Scott shook his head.

"From the day of you turned 18, maybe a time or two before that, I've had a lot of confusion when it comes to you. I'm not a big talker or the assessor of my feelings, but at that time I didn't like what being around you told me about myself."

"I know. I'm not sure what would have happened if people didn't just assume I was gay. It wasn't ever really a question and it seemed like everyone just knew...I've only recently understood that to be a good thing because hiding wasn't an option." Scott shrugged.

"It's probably because you were and are so very pretty."

Scott punched Bailey in the arm playfully. "You always say that. I used to think you were such an asshole for saying it."

"I was being honest then and I'm being honest now. You've buffed up a bit and the scruff adds another dimension to your look, but you've still got a sweet face."

"What? Like a woman?"

"No. Just like a pretty boy back then and a very hot guy as we speak. I did say it in jest when I was younger, just playing with you, but it was true." It was Bailey's turn to feel the warmth of embarrassment. It was difficult saying things he'd normally just hear in his head, but he'd done some damage on his way out of town years ago and it was way past time to clean this up.

"So after we got off you asked me very politely to move and then drove me home. You didn't fuss or fight or argue with me. I just never saw you again, until you tried to break up a fight in the middle of a bar while I was on duty." Scott had put the question to him with a slight smile and a bit of sass but Bailey could tell that's what he was the most hurt about.

"Like I said, I didn't like how I was feeling and what it said about me. I wasn't ready to be...attracted to a man. I figured it was because I'd never—"

"Never what?" Scott frowned as he asked.

"Um, I'd never been dumped. Maybe I was heartbroken." Bailey wasn't ready to let that out of the bag and he didn't even know why it was important any more but it was.

"So she dumped you and you never saw her again and you did the same to me?" Scott didn't look like he was so hot on how this conversation was going, but Bailey had decided that from now on he was going to live his truth, whatever it was. He had men who hadn't returned from their time as enlisted personnel and he could have been among them, but he wasn't and he was going to live to the fullest.

He grabbed Scott's hand. "It probably seems like that, but I didn't even put that together. Was I running? Yes, I was and for that I'm sorry."

Scott pulled back his hand and scooted back a few inches on the couch. He returned his gaze to the television that wasn't on and Bailey wondered what was going on in his mind.

"Looks like you're pissed and that I understand, but I've got to ask...what happens now?"

Chapter 10

"WHAT HAPPENS NOW?" Scott repeated like a stupid parrot. It was hard to believe that he was even getting this kind of closure. The man had been a part of his life forever and then poof he was gone. He had gotten the man out of his mind as much as he could and then poof he was back. "You don't even know what you're doing. Have you been with a man before?" He turned back toward Bailey because he wanted to see his expression when he answered the question.

Bailey shook his head. "The night with you crossed my mind a time or two and I thought about trying something with a guy when I was hit on, but it never went further than a thought. I went to The Male Box to once and for all figure out if I had a thing for guys, although the fact that I had questions had me thinking that something is there."

"What did you find out when you went to The Male Box?"

"I found that you throw a hell of a right hook." Bailey smiled, and it was hard for Scott not to give him one in return but he quelled it. The deep voice Scott had missed so much quieted down to almost a whisper. "I also found out that I'm still very attracted to you."

Scott had turned from sitting on the couch facing him to facing the television. He wasn't going to focus on the inner teen that was so happy about the last sentence he wanted to bounce on the couch with happiness. Scott was older and wiser now, so he had to get real with his questions. "So you're in the experimental stage?"

"I guess?" Bailey answered his question with another and Scott knew he was staring at him, he could feel the warm gaze like a caress.

"I'm not really good at being the subject of the gay experiment that, but I can help out like I said I would. It's only right since you protected my ass all through school."

"So for protecting your ass you're going to let me fuck it too?" Bailey's joking tone lifted the mood of the room and Scott held on to it like a lifeline. If he was going to get through this with just minor injuries he was going to have to take all of this lightly.

"Ha...If anyone will be getting fucked it will be you. I don't bottom for anyone, but it doesn't have to just be about either one of us sticking our cocks in ass. There are other things we can do, but I'm only going to be a starter. I'm bending my personal rules about experimental straight men for you." Scott chanced a look in Bailey's direction. He appeared to be thinking this over.

"Are you saying I'm a one and done?"

"Well, since we've already done one and I'm suggesting this, I'm going to say it's not quite that, but this isn't an exclusive thing. If you see someone that draws your interest, then feel free to see them. The same goes for me."

Bailey pulled Scott across his lap and it took him a bit off guard. Sometimes he forgot how big Bailey was, but he quickly remembered how much he liked feeling securely held tight against the large man's body.

"So if we're here together and neither of us are attached, then this would be alright?" Bailey kissed him just like he liked it. Hard and devouring. His tongue was demanding he respond and when he answered back Bailey moaned low and deep. The sound wrapped around his cock like a physical touch so much it was hard not to pump his hips to get more friction. Bailey broke the kiss and they both sounded like they'd run a quick sprint. It took a minute for Scott to remember he'd been asked a question.

"Sure."

"So with this experimentation?" Bailey was playful and arousing, but Scott needed to remember what this was.

"Yeah?"

"Will I actually get to see your cock this time? Each time we've fooled around there has been intense rubbing and a huge sticky mess in my pants, but no actual skin was viewed or touched." Bailey rubbed his large hands up and down Scott's back.

There was something Scott really liked about big men. He didn't know or care what that said about him, but he felt very protected. "Is this you saying you want to see my cock?"

"No. This is me saying I want to taste your cock and I want to see you come. I've never seen that sight and I think about it constantly. I've missed it twice, but I won't miss it again."

"You never have to ask me. Just help yourself." Scott liked that they were getting back to playful banter until he found himself flipped onto his back with Bailey pulling down his sweat pants. Although it seemed like he kept a half chub around the man all the time, he couldn't remember a time when his cock was as hard as it was now. Self-doubt wasn't a usual companion of his either, but that fucker had taken up residence inside his head and was now unpacking his shit like he wanted to stay a while. He'd never had any complaints about the size or function of his cock, but he was actually feeling a bit anxious about both when Bailey took him into his hand.

"I've seen porn, but this is my first time actually doing this. Tell me if I fuck it up." Bailey was pumping his hand up and down Scott's shaft slowly. Staring at it like it was going to do something magical and it was. All the magic inside was going to spurt onto his face if he didn't give him a minute.

Scott put his hand over Bailey's. "Hold on a second."

"I've been waiting forever. You said to help yourself...are you changing your mind?"

"N...no." It was hard to think let alone have a conversation when his cock was engulfed in Bailey's large fist.

"Good." Bailey licked the head of his cock like it was a delicate ice cream cone and he did it with a sense of awe that came through loud and clear.

Keeping his hips from moving was what Scott was supposed to be doing, but it was a tough task. The next lick had been less tentative, but just watching Harold Fucking Bailey holding his cock in his hand, staring at it intently and working his way up to do more was more arousing than the most talented cock sucker could ever be.

"I've wanted to do this since you pulled your dripping wet body out of the pool on your 18th birthday. I've thought about doing what I'm doing so often it feels like I should know what to do by now." Bailey looked up at his face when he spoke to him, but watching his mouth so close to his cock wasn't something that was going to make him able to let Bailey do what he wanted. Scott was at an nine plus on the scale of arousal and his balls were drawn up tight.

"Why don't we take off our clothes, then I can see you too?" Scott thought that idea might buy him a few minutes and he could use it to cool off a bit. It probably wouldn't be enough to ease the pressure that had built up in his balls, but it could give him a slight break from the intenseness of the moment.

"I don't want to let you go." Bailey looked into Scott's eyes as he opened his mouth and wrapped his lips around the head of Scott's cock. He took in a little more until more than half of his shaft had disappeared inside the warm cavern of his mouth.

Scott's hips bucked and he let his head fall back. He really wanted to close his eyes, but the sensation seemed to be even more intense with his eyes closed.

"Look at me, Scott. I want to see your face when you come. I've waited for this shit so long it's like this moment isn't real." Bailey had lifted his head away from Scott's cock to talk, but the steady, rhythmic hand strokes had continued and Scott gave into the desire to fuck his buddy's fist. He met the man's thrusts and could feel his abs quivering as his orgasm drew closer.

"Fuuuuck, Bailey." There was no way this wasn't going to end with one of the biggest loads Scott had ever blown and gone was his desire to go slow for the newbie. With one foot braced on the couch and the other on the floor, he lifted his hips to get his cock deeper into Bailey's hot mouth. "Unless you want your mouth full you'd better move."

Bailey kept his gaze glued to Scott's face and grunted. The way he remained latched onto his cock Scott could only assume he wasn't going to move. Just watching his cock go in and out of Bailey's mouth was going to push him over the edge, but the intense concentration while he sucked him off and the beard hair that slid against him with each downward stroke was hiking his response higher.

"I'm serious, man. Fuck!" Scott looked down and swore the man was trying not to smile and the glint in his eye reminded him of how sexy he sounded when he laughed. His body tightened and all his muscles froze as his cock spurted hard. Scott's abs contracted and released so quickly it took his breath away. The shouts and moans that filled the room were so loud and hard to hold back they almost mocked him. Scott closed his eyes and tried to catch his breath.

"That was pretty hot, Scotty." Bailey had licked his cock clean and was sitting between his legs.

"Don't call me Scotty." He opened up one eye and closed it again after he got a look at the pride and happiness on Bailey's face.

"Dude, I'm sitting here with a gut full of your swimmers. I should be able to call you whatever I want." Bailey leaned in and licked the space right beside Scott's belly button.

Scott opened his eyes and found himself face to face with Bailey.

"I finally watched you come and fuck, that was hot. We can take this however you want to take it, but know that for you I'm willing to take whatever you give me."

Looking at Bailey's face as he begged for crumbs did something to his resolve, but he couldn't give in. This man wasn't just a regular man trying to experiment with his sexuality. This was his Bailey. *His* Bailey. He didn't know how he was going to survive this when it was over, but he wanted to give the man as much as he could.

"Let me up."

He watched the troubled expression cloud Bailey's face as he got up off him. Scott stood up and placed his hand on Bailey's cock. It was so massive it was hard to believe all that didn't split his pants.

Bailey laid his hand over his and drew in a deep breath. "Let's just be done for now. You look like you're headed into a battle with yourself. I know how that feels because I've been there. I don't want you to have that with me."

"I don't want to leave you like this when you've done so well by me."

"That's not how I want you. I want you to be all in and do whatever we do because you want to, because I wanted to taste your cock for years. I'm happy, but you're conflicted."

"I'm not—"

"Honesty only," Bailey said as he backed away from Scott.

Scott couldn't help but look longingly at Bailey's cock, because he really wanted to try the man out. He couldn't count the times he'd thought about being on his knees and taking Bailey in his mouth or deep within his body. He'd said he didn't bottom for anyone and he didn't anymore, but he knew if Bailey wanted him he'd give in. "I may be a little conflicted."

"That's better. I'm going to head up to my room and get some sleep and you think about what you're passing up." Bailey smiled as he rubbed Scott's hand down to his balls and back to the tip of his cock before removing both of their hands and backing away. It was the smile that made Scott's heart speed up like it always had and he shook his head at his friends teasing.

"Hey, I offered."

"And I appreciate it. Offer again when it doesn't look like you're being forced to walk the plank." The smile was teasing, but Scott still felt like shit for making the man take care of that himself, especially when he really wanted in on that.

Scott just nodded as Bailey walked toward the stairs.

"Stop looking at me like that. I may want to play with you or experiment as you say, but I know how to take care of this."

"You're an ass." Scott laughed at Bailey and it was like it was the first good laugh he'd had in days.

"I made you laugh. A deep belly laugh and I'm satisfied with that." Bailey was halfway up the stairs before he stopped and turned back. "Thanks for letting me stay here and thanks for trying to work through whatever you're working through on my account. If I were a better man I'd just let it go, but I'm hoping you'll take a chance with me."

Scott nodded and the sincerity in Bailey's voice touched him. Fuck, this is what he was afraid of. The man turned and walked the rest of the way up the stairs and Scott heard the door to his room open and close. He knew he'd better get to his room and get to bed before he heard a squeaking bed, a growl or moan because whatever was holding him back wouldn't survive that. He'd be in the man's bedroom begging for him to forget any conflict he may have and fuck his face like he does in his dreams.

Chapter 11

"YOU'RE DOING MUCH BETTER than I thought you'd be doing." Honey had packed up her gear that she'd just had all over the living room. Bailey had to give her credit she gave a good workout for his arm and listening to her talk and joke while they'd done it had made it less painful than it typically was for him. It also didn't hurt that Honey had asked Scott to come down to watch a part of what she was doing in case he wanted to help out on the days she didn't come. It had been a few days since the hotness on the couch had happened and gave Bailey more information about himself than he'd have gathered from a month's worth of trips to The Male Box, but Scott had pretty much reverted back to the slightly standoffish demeanor he'd had before the episode. He was attentive to Honey during the instruction and helped a bit with the stretching when he was called upon, but he was doing the bare minimum. Most days, Scott's behavior made Bailey think there was some sort of penalty his friend had to pay if he looked directly into Bailey's face because that didn't happen at all.

Honey handed each of them a sheet explaining the exercises that were supposed to stretch and strengthen Bailey's arm. He was trying hard not to study Scott as he read the paper. For someone who was often called aloof by his lovers, Bailey was finding it hard to be nonchalant whenever Scott was around.

"Thanks," Bailey said, making an effort to study the paper Honey had given him.

"No problem." Honey stood up and surveyed the room for any more of her stuff when there was a knock on the door. A few seconds later, Ollie walked in.

"Looks like I found the party. Hey there, Honey." Ollie carried in a case of beer and he spoke to Honey without looking at her. He also had a bag that Bailey knew would be full of food. It was like the man was trying to make up for shoving him off on his brother. When he didn't bring food over he sent it over.

"Dude, you've got to stop feeding us. It's got to be costing you a mint," Bailey yelled as he walked through the living room and disappeared into the kitchen.

"I'll do what I want. My friend is back and I'm trying to let him know how glad I am to have him." Ollie could only be heard as he shuffled things around. Scott stood up and walked into the kitchen with his brother.

"I'm getting ready to leave," Honey said, "but make sure you keep up with your stretches and exercises. I'll check up on you tomorrow and we can plan when I come back." Honey kissed him on the cheek right when Scott walked back into the room.

"Honey, Ollie brought more food than a small country could eat in one sitting. Stay and have something with us." Scott's grin was open and infectious. It made Bailey wish he was the one who could make the man look like that. It seemed like Scott was always rushing out when he came in.

"No, but thank you. I'm sure you guys have lots to talk about and need some space. Plus, I've got a few errands I need to run."

"Want some company? We can let these two bond without us," Scott said like he was conspiring a heist.

Honey looked at him like she was confused, but caught herself after a few seconds and put on her patented smile. "Nah, I think I'll do them alone."

Bailey looked between the both of them and wondered what was going on. Honey gave Scott a hug and picked up her things. Scott picked up the heaviest box and followed her to the car. Bailey was going to think that one over later, but he had to talk to Ollie.

"Don't do any of this guilt shit with me. I'm fine staying here with Scott," Bailey said as he walked into the kitchen.

"What? A guy can't bring his best buddy and his brother a bit of grub?" Scott was laying out the food along with the plates and cups.

"You've done this quite often and it's not necessary. You don't have to try to make anything up to me. I'm fine here."

Ollie slumped down in one of the kitchen seats like the starch in his spine had given way. "I hate that you left so abruptly way back when and now of all times I have a visitor so you can't stay with me. I just wanted to make sure you knew how glad I am to have you back in town."

Bailey punched his friend's arm playfully. "Of course I know you're glad to have me back. I'm glad to be back." Bailey looked at Ollie and wondered why he'd left and stayed away for so long, but then the reason walked through the door.

"I'm going to go out for a bit." Scott looked like a bug on a hook, and he wondered if his brother noticed he was trying to get away from the both of them.

"What? No way. I brought all this food because even though you're smaller than both of us, you eat double the portion. You've got to stay." Ollie moved closer to Scott and pulled him in for a half hug, half tussle like wrestling move before Scott pushed him away with a laugh.

"You two haven't had a lot of time together and I don't mind leaving. I've been in the house more than I usually am trying to make sure Bailey doesn't need anything and it would do me good to get out."

"What I need a babysitter?" Bailey said with a laugh, but deep down he wondered if that's what Scott thought he was responsible to do. "I'm a grown man who can put up a recon station in record time. I brush my teeth and comb my hair all by myself. I think I'm old enough to take care of myself and you."

Scott's face pinkened a bit and Bailey wondered if he should be enjoying the man's discomfort as much as he was. It was probably because it had been hard to tie the man down for a conversation that didn't sound like he was trying to look out for Bailey's needs around the house. Not the hot sex, or just intimacy needs, more like the needs to find shit around the house.

"Come on." Ollie elbowed his brother once more and although he didn't agree he did make his way to the table and sat down assessing the food his brother had set out.

There wasn't a lot of talking from Scott but Bailey thought it was cool how he and Ollie had just settled into conversation just like old times. There weren't any tense silences or need to walk on egg shells he could just open his mouth and talk.

"So I see Honey has been coming back around. What's going on with her?" Ollie asked after everyone's plates were clear and they just lingered around the table.

"Nothing. She's a physical therapist and is working out my shoulder. I was going to turn her down and just find a local facility, but she was adamant about helping me and she has all the stuff I need in the bags she brings." Bailey wasn't sure who turned on the awkward but he was feeling it washing over him.

"I think she's into you, man. She's probably eating her heart out over letting you go." Ollie took a swig of his beer and set it down rather firmly on the table.

"I don't think that's the case, but even so, it's been a long time. Why do you seem so upset by it?" Bailey said to Ollie, but then glanced over at Scott, who had a look on his face that implied he knew the answer.

"She's the one who started all this shit in the first place." Ollie got up from the table. "The game is about to be on, let's clean up this mess and then take these to the living room."

Bailey was going to have to take back what he'd said about him and Ollie being like they'd been before, but he refused to walk on egg shells with anyone else in this house. It was bad enough he did it with Scott.

"I can't believe you are blaming Honey. Are upset about something that didn't involve you and that happened so long ago?"

"Didn't involve me, huh?" Ollie huffed out as he wiped down the table.

Bailey brought out three beers to the living room and waited for the guys to follow. It was taking them a good deal of time to walk out of the room that was clean when he left and he wondered if Scott was talking to him about something. They walked out and sat down on the two reclining chairs on either side of the couch Bailey had chosen to sit in. Ollie stood up and got the remote control from the television and returned to his seat before he turned on the game he'd wanted to watch.

"Dude, that break up changed my life. Both of our lives. We were going to be firemen with the city, get an apartment and go to the community college after high school. You were on board with this plan until Honey broke up with you. I was away with the Mountie scouts summer program and when I returned, you were gone. All I got was a note that said some shit about your plans had changed and you were going to the military." Ollie glanced his way briefly when he'd finished talking but for the most part he'd kept his eyes on the television.

Bailey felt like shit remembering that. It was true that he'd left in a hurry and he could see why the man would think that Honey was the reason he left. It was some of the reason, but there had been more. He'd been a selfish asshole to leave without more than what he gave to Ollie, but the times he'd called the man throughout the years he'd never really sounded like he was upset so Bailey didn't think it meant as much as it clearly did. Damn it.

"I was selfish and dealing with shit I didn't know how to handle. I wish I could've gotten my head out of my ass to realize I wasn't the only one affected." Bailey was happy to see Ollie's patented huge smile.

"You're not normally the dumb ass, Bailey. That's usually the Callahan Boys claim to fame, but not to worry, just don't do that shit again. It's good having you back."

They all turned their attention to the men running up and down the field for the pigskin with a bit of noise from Scott and the color commentary coming from Ollie about the players that was actually pretty entertaining.

"Hey, Bailey, I know this girl who would be perfect for you," Ollie said during one of the commercial breaks.

Bailey turned to look at Scott, who was trying not to look panicked and wouldn't take his eyes away from the program on the screen.

"Well, since I've been back in town I've been—"

"Who's the lady? I'm sure if you think it's a good match for Bailey he should probably give her a try," Scott spoke up and Bailey was shocked since it didn't seem like the man had said more than a few words in a clip since this get together started.

Bailey looked between the two brothers. One face was filled with excitement and the other cautiously blank. He studied the blank expression on Scott's face and could see that he didn't want his brother to know about the things Bailey was trying to work out for himself. Maybe it was a good idea to meet some new people. Would something happen? Probably not, but since he was still investigating what could it hurt to share a meal with his best friend and the woman he'd picked out.

"Okay, sure. What could it hurt?"

"Famous last words," Ollie said with a chuckle. "But since I made the date for tonight, I'm not going to complain that I didn't have to do more than ask."

"Tonight?" Bailey sat up and turned to his friend who was now acting like the game on the television held the answers to all the questions of the universe.

"Yep," Ollie looked over quickly and then returned his gaze to the screen. "I figured I could get you to come out, but I didn't know if it would hold. Didn't want you to think that hard about it."

"Why such a hard press to get me a date?"

"I just want to get you back involved in the community." The shrug should have told Bailey that this was just a casual thing but it made it seem there was more to it.

"What I'm hearing is that if you can get me hooked up into a woman then I have less of a chance to leave. Is that right?"

Ollie took a deep breath and then a long drink from his beer. "There may be something to that, but really I just wanted you to meet someone nice so you can start living your civilian life on the wild side."

It was a good thing Bailey was a mild mannered soul because if he was a hot head like either one of the two brothers used to be, he'd be pissed at everyone in the room. Scott for pushing him off on some chick and for tiptoeing around him since Bailey had performed his first blowjob, and for Ollie for heavy handedly trying to keep him in town with some woman he didn't know.

"What time are we supposed to be leaving?" Bailey got up and walked toward his room. He didn't really want to be around Scott right now and after the physical therapy, a large meal and a few drinks he wanted some time to himself.

"It's not until tonight. There's no need to rush off. We can watch a few more games," Ollie said with a frown on his usually smiling face.

"I'm going to take a nap. Something else I didn't do much of in the military. I'll be down in a few hours refreshed, clean and ready to meet Ms. Wonderful." Bailey hoped the smile didn't feel like the sneer that was inside him. He went upstairs before anyone else could try to get him back into the conversation.

This whole thing with Scott was making him loopy. If this was something he was going to try then maybe he should just forget about his best friend's younger brother being anything but a roommate to him. His stomach didn't seem to like that choice as it rolled like the beer, food and good times didn't agree with him.

Bailey made it to the top of the stairs and heard Ollie, who was the world's worst whisperer. "What's going on with you two?"

"Absolutely nothing worth talking about." Scott's tone and words were level and honest. Maybe that was the way things really were. If Bailey had been on the fence before he'd been knocked off and ass out on the grass beneath him. It wasn't a problem. He wasn't going to run this time, but he was going to get answers but without Scott.

Chapter 12

SCOTT HAD TALKED HIMSELF out of coming here twenty times, but that twenty-first time had been too hard to ignore. He was breaking a few of his own rules. The 'Don't come to the bar when you're not working' rule and the much more important, 'Don't fucking chase Bailey' rule had been blown to smithereens with one late night visit to The Male Box. It hadn't seemed like the best thing to do when he put on his clothes immediately after Mark had called to tell him about a patron of the bar, nor when he hopped into his car and raced here like he was in a competition for the street racing finals.

He stood against the wall, watching a few choice men try to engage what Scott's heart screamed was his was the worst thing to do. When he'd first found this bar, he'd slept around with a lot of the patrons of the bar but that was then and this is now. These days, if he wanted companionship, there were other places to go that didn't add to his financial health at the end of the month.

"I knew you'd show up." Mark walked up beside him and spoke up. It should have startled him, but the man had been doing that to him since he'd met him.

"That's why you called, wasn't it? To get me to prove to you that I'm still into him?" Scott didn't look at Mark because if he saw that patented smirk that usually graced his face when he was proven right he might just fight him regardless of how much the man towered over him.

"Hey..." Mark nudged him with his elbow so Scott looked over at him. "I didn't call you so I could rub the fact your guy was here looking interested in other people. I called because the man looked like he was hurting and trying to figure shit out. I know people. It comes with being a bartender for such a long time."

Scott could almost feel the sincerity in Mark's words, but that didn't take the sick feeling away from him. In fact, his stomach got more twisted as one of the dancers Mark had brought in to increase business walked over and took the seat next to Bailey. The dancer's name was Eric. He was hot as all shit and the man flashed a smile and a good bit of skin at Bailey. Scott would swear that almost everyone in the club had tried to put the moves on the guy to no avail and here he was sitting practically hip to hip with his Bailey.

"Holy Shit," Mark said with a laugh beside him. "What the fuck kind of pheromones does that guy have? He's turned you into a shy wall flower and made Mr. Belle of the Ball become a hunter instead of being hunted."

"That's hilarious," Scott said dryly. He pushed himself off the wall and turned to the door.

"Wait." Mark grabbed Scott as he walked by. "Who the fuck are you anymore? One of the reasons you were so fun to be around when you were younger is because you were such a fighter. I'm looking at you and I can almost smell how much you want him. Why leave?"

"Some things just aren't worth fighting for." Scott pulled his arm away from Mark who raised his hands in surrender.

"You keep telling yourself that. It's going to make cold company when Eric is sitting in your living room helping Bailey find out how hot it is to fulfill all the fantasies and dreams he's had all this time to cultivate. I don't know what brought him here when he has you at home, but whatever it is I wanted to give you the chance to fix it." Mark turned and backed away from Scott. "But, point taken. I'll never call you again when your Bailey shows up."

Scott watched him walk away and knew he had no right to be angry at anyone but himself. He'd pushed Bailey away because he didn't think he'd be able to handle how it would be when the man worked out whatever he was trying to work through and went back to his normally scheduled programming. It was dumb to be upset because he was looking into other people to get his questions answered.

Bailey and Eric had rainbow shots lined up in front of them. Different alcohols in the seven shades of the rainbow and the two men were acting so chummy it was hard to believe they'd just met tonight. They seemed to be talking between downing the colored shots and Scott decided to leave them to it. He was going to walk away. Scott put one foot in front of the other but found himself standing in the small space between the men he was supposed to be walking away from.

"Hey, Scott," Eric said when finished his shot, set his glass down and turned to say something to Bailey.

"Eric," Scott said with a nod. Although he had walked over to where these two men looked like they were having a good time getting to know each other he had nothing else to say, but he wanted to know what Bailey would do.

"Want to sit down with us?" Eric started to get up from his seat.

"I'm sure Scott is just passing through." Bailey held on to Eric's arm lightly as he tried to stand.

Eric looked at Bailey for a few minutes and then back at Scott with a sigh. "I have to get back to the stage for a few but keep an eye on my drinks. I'll be back with more guesses on my next break." Eric smiled as Bailey let the man go and then turned his attention back to his drinks.

"Can I have a water?" Bailey called out to the bartender.

"Come get it yourself. You are working here now so you know where the glasses are." Ira was a five foot five blond dynamo that had more energy than everyone in the room put together and knew more trivia than anyone Scott had ever met or heard of. He walked off while looking at Bailey as he walked away, but then returned quickly with his water. "Last call is in an hour, so I don't want you and your fine ass back here taking my tips."

Ira stood in front of them and looked between the both of them. Scott thought about what to add at this moment but came up blank.

"What can I get for you, hottie?" Ira said as he wiped down the bar. He'd called him that since the first day they'd met and the man decided Scott looked like him but with a darker complexion and hair.

"Nothing, man, I'm just going to say a couple things to my buddy here and then go." Scott pointed his thumb at Bailey.

Ira smiled as he studied them. "Well, if you change your mind, let me know." The dynamo walked away more slowly than Scott had ever seen or maybe he was just in a rush say something to Bailey and change the way things were going between them.

Scott opened his mouth and hoped he was going to say the right thing.

"I get it, Scott. You used to have a thing for me when you were younger, but now you don't. No hard feelings," Bailey said, looking into the shot glasses, but picking up the glass of water and drinking three-fourths of it down in a few swallows.

"That's not what I was going to say." Scott turned to Bailey and almost caught his breath when the green eyes he had remembered for years glanced at him. It took a few minutes to get himself together to say what he wanted. Scott picked up Bailey's water and took a drink and he heard the beginning of Bailey's deep, soft chuckle.

Scott put the drink down and looked up and down the bar. It really was late and it was the find and fuck hour. If magic, in the way of an orgasm, was going to happen as a duet instead of the solo five knuckle shuffle tonight these yokels would get started making their deals in the next few minutes.

"Well, then what were you going to say because I was sitting here with someone who had no hang ups or whatever you're feeling about spending a bit of time with me." Bailey looked back into his drink, but quickly looked back at him like he decided to put him on the spot.

Scott cleared his throat as he looked around to see who was paying attention to them. It didn't seem like anyone but Ira had focused on the two of them. The bartender was trying hard to seem like he was not interested in what was going on at the end of the bar, but he was betraying that by cleaning the hell out of that one glass while staying still and mastering his art of information by peripheral vision. "I don't really want to talk here as it's the place that we both work, but I will if you want."

"As long as whatever you have to say isn't going to end with you telling me some bullshit and then you scurry around being everywhere that I'm not." Bailey had a slight smile on his face, but Scott recognized the look as one of frustration as there was no joy in that grimace.

"It's not," Scott said as he stood up. "I'll drive you home."

"I haven't had that much to drink. Come on, Scott. I'm 6 foot 3 and my scale tips higher than 245 pounds. A few drinks aren't enough to put me close to the legal limit that would make me unqualified for me to drive."

Scott stood up and moved behind Bailey's chair. "Hand over your keys or prepare to be frisked until I find them."

"Are you serious?" Bailey turned his head to look at Scott.

"I'm as serious as I've ever been. There is no way we get this far and you get into an accident. Ollie wouldn't ever forgive me if that happened." Scott closed his eyes briefly and held his breath, but Bailey didn't say anything about that statement and Scott knew he was going to have to get his emotions in order or who the hell knew what else he'd spouted out of his mouth.

Bailey moved out of his stool away from Scott, put on his jacket, pulled out his wallet and put a good number of bills on the bar and walked toward the door. Scott had no idea why he was so puzzled, but he didn't think Bailey would give in that easy. He followed him out the door and didn't bother looking around. At this point he'd already shown that he was full of fucks to give when it came to this man and he didn't want anyone to ask any questions.

Scott had learned a lot in his time as a police officer about people and anticipating their moves, but spending time trying to figure out what he was going to say and how this was going to work between him and Bailey must have totally thrown him off. He looked up and saw he was following the large man to the alley behind the bar.

"What the—"

Bailey spun around and pushed Scott against the wall. "No."

Shaking his head, he tried to recall what Bailey was asking because he didn't recall asking him anything since they'd come outside. "No, what?"

"I'm not giving you my keys, and I'm driving home."

Scott couldn't believe this. He knew the man was probably tipsy but he didn't know if Bailey was belligerent after a few drinks or just playful. "It's not going to happen. I know you think you're stronger than I am, but I'll whoop your ass and put you in cuffs before you can finish your next sentence."

"I don't believe that." Bailey's eyes crinkled as he smiled and it brought the heat Scott was feeling down a few notches.

"Are you playing with me?"

"You offered to do something if I said no to your order. I didn't want you to do it inside the bar, but now I'm wondering if you'd actually go through with it so I'm telling you no out here." Bailey was towering over Scott.

"I'm not like I was before you left. I can take you, but it's not going to be pretty. You're a big guy so unless you feel like getting roughed up I suggest we get in the car and go home."

Bailey moved closer. "If you want my keys, officer then you'll have to find and take them."

Scott could see the look on Bailey's face because of the light that came around the corner and shone in Bailey's direction. The man was breathing deep and slightly more labored than he had been previously and he wondered what kind of fantasies Bailey stroked off too because this seemed to be doing it for him. Scott used one of the techniques Bailey had taught him years ago. He got low and stood up quickly, knocking the wind out of the large man towering over him before pushing him back. Scott worked his way behind Bailey and pushed him against the wall, kicking his legs so they were spread apart as he took out his cuffs. Bailey put up a fight as Scott cuffed the arm that was resting against the wall and pulled it behind him.

"Huh, I wasn't expecting you to actually have the cuffs on you, but I wasn't expecting you to hit me in the diaphragm either, but I should have. I taught you that. Didn't I?"

"When you're in the disadvantage you have to use what you can and maybe you did." Scott was a little winded, but he wasn't sure if it was because he was grappling with a large man in an alleyway or because he was doing it with his cock harder than it had been since he was a teen waking up in the middle of a wet dream. "Hand me your other wrist."

Bailey waited a few seconds and when he didn't move Scott figured he must want more. He wrenched the cuffed arm, he had higher than it had been before, but not too much as he didn't want to fuck up the man's good shoulder. Bailey brought the arm down and Scott was glad because he was holding the pressure pretty high on the captured arm, but Scott wasn't going to back down. He'd been raised with the boy that became this man and he knew how his mind worked. Well, he used to know how his mind worked.

"Bring your arm back to me with your thumb up." Scott said, trying to anticipate Bailey's next move. It wasn't his plan to fuck the man in the alley, but the adrenaline mixed with being with Harold *Fucking* Bailey was too much. Bailey was bringing his hand down slowly but leaned back and cupped Scott's cock and curled around his balls through the denim pants he wore.

"Bailey. *Fuck.*" Scott closed his eyes and breathed in. He was thankful that this wasn't where they put the trash because that would mean it would smell like hell back here and there would be more of an opportunity for someone to find them playing whatever the hell they were playing outside the club.

"Search me." The voice was quiet, needy and so hot it caused warmth to radiate through his body. Bailey squeezed his cock hard enough to make Scott want to whimper. Not in pain, but with pleasure. He held his hand just right and he wondered if Bailey had more experience than he was letting on.

"Place your hands against the wall and don't move it until I say so," Scott said in his most commanding voice and could hear his cuffs swinging to hit the brick wall because Bailey had gotten them up there so quickly. He stood so close to Bailey that he'd have to feel his hard on against his back and he rubbed his full thick cock against the seam of Bailey's ass. "If you want to play, Bailey all you had to do is ask."

"I did that in every way, but words. You said you needed your space and I'm trying to respect that, but don't think I don't know you ran over here because you thought I was trying to 'experiment' as you say, with someone else."

Scott slowed his rubbing and thought about what he wanted to admit and what he'd been thinking of saying. He opened his mouth and tried to measure the words that exited but in the end, nothing came out and he closed his mouth.

"Deny it and I'm done. I get you've got some hang up when it comes to me, but you don't get to stop anything I'm doing just because you don't want me playing with someone else. I'm not a bone to play tug of war with," Bailey said over his shoulder.

"I was going to say that I'm not denying that Mark called me and told me you were here and the sharks were swimming around you." Scott had his hands on Bailey's hips but there was nothing professional about the way he was standing. His cock was still in contact with Bailey's body and only a few layers of clothes separated him from the warm skin he ached to lick...suck...bite.

"I don't think they were sharks and I wasn't in any danger, but since that wasn't a denial, I guess you can continue your search. Carry on, officer."

Chapter 13

BAILEY WAS IN NO WAY too drunk to drive, but he was enjoying watching Scott get all worked up... in more than one way. The date he'd gone on had been a bust, just like he knew it would be, and while Candy was just as sweet as her name implied, he had absolutely no interest in her.

"Spread your legs more." Scott's voice was raspy like he'd not talked for a long while.

Just words like that coming from Scott made it impossible to calm himself down. It had been a fantasy of his to make out against a wall in an alleyway with Scott since he learned the man was a cop. 'Spread your legs more' was definitely in the script for when he had his cock in his hand and his thoughts on the man behind him. He did what was asked of him and wondered how far Scott would go.

"Did you scope this place out earlier?" Scott asked as he slowly put his arms around Bailey's body to feel at his belt buckle before sliding his hands around the perimeter of his waist.

Trying to think while living his fantasy was difficult, to say the least. "Yes. I saw this place and heard there are no cameras and practically no traffic. I didn't think I'd get a chance to use it, but it's good to know your surroundings."

A grunt was all Scott offered as an answer to that. He was moving his hands up over Bailey's pecs from the back and it almost felt like a hug he was moving so slow. Scott returned his hands to Bailey's belt and then did the same movement, but slid his arms up his back and around his collar.

"It must take you forever to frisk someone." Bailey was enjoying the contact but he was not as big on the teasing touches. He wanted the hard, rough touch he'd imagine that would come with being with a man. Dishing it out was easy for him because he controlled the pace, and he'd often gone this slow, but he had been hard since Scott walked up and he could smell the tension scented pheromones radiating from him.

"Are you rushing me, Bailey?" Scott's voice was deeper and smokier than it usually was and Bailey pushed out his ass to bump him. Hurry him along. Something. It must have worked because Scott patted his way down one leg and then the other before coming up to feel around his crotch in one sliding move from the back. "What do we have here?"

It was a classic porn line and Bailey couldn't help but chuckle a bit. "I don't know officer, but if it's illegal, then it's not mine."

"Possession is nine-tenths of the law." Scott moved his hand along the outline of his cock firmly creating a sweet friction that drew his balls up tight and made the fit of his jeans just that much more uncomfortable. It was almost impossible not to thrust against his hand. "I'm going to have to check this out."

Scott opened up the belt, released some of the buttons on his fly and Bailey let go a loud sigh.

"I'm sure that feels better, doesn't it, buddy?"

"It does, officer, thanks for your help." Bailey wanted to watch what Scott was doing, but the lighting was spotty and he was facing a wall so it was all shadows. This whole situation had him hyperalert. His body was sensitive regularly, but not like this. Scott reaching into his shorts and bringing his cock and balls through the flap in the front of his underwear was so pleasurable it was almost painful.

"I do what I can to help those in need." Scott finally got Bailey out the way he wanted him to be because Scott gripped Bailey's cock the way he imagined he gripped himself. Firm and no nonsense at the base. Bailey almost whimpered, but he didn't. He held that breath and waited.

The first stroke was slow and Bailey let the breath he was holding out in a slow hiss as he attempted to keep himself together.

"So getting jerked off by an officer in a dirty alleyway does it for you, Bailey?"

The words should have been embarrassing, but they weren't. Bailey looked down at Scott's hand gripping his cock while he stood off balance with his hands against the brick wall. "Yes."

"I wouldn't have figured you for it, but now that I know... I want to make it worth your while."

Just hearing what this was should have made him cringe, but the way it was spoken was like a caress more than a reprimand. It's possible he was reading this wrong, but he was too amped up to do more than grunt out a response as Scott's movements grew tighter and faster as he ground his hard cock against Bailey's ass.

"It seems you like it too," Bailey said as he started fucking into his friend's tight fist.

"Oh, there's not much about you I don't like, but I imagine you know that. You've always known that." Scott's strokes were rougher than Bailey would have done for himself, but it was gritty and dirty like their location and fuck, if the fact he was with Scott wasn't hiking this experience up to extreme proportions.

"I used to be able to set the sunrise on it, but lately I'm not too sure," Bailey huffed out. He could feel Scott's hard cock against his ass as he ground against him and he was surrounded by the smaller man. He put his hand on top of the one Scott was stroking his cock to help moderate, but he didn't know what he wanted...to draw this out or to come right now.

"Move your hand away from your cock. You may touch it when I tell you too." Scott growled from behind him.

That shouldn't have made his balls draw up tight or his body tense up, but the authority in the tone was exactly the way he'd imagined when he pulled his own cock thinking of something like this. He moved his hand behind him to the spot Scott was rubbing his cock against him and held his hand against the hardness in Scott's pants. There wasn't more he could do with his body seized up like it was preparing to shatter.

"You're almost there, Bailey. Fuck my hand and come."

The words and the tugs made it hard for him to breath and impossible to answer, but his body decided to obey the command. Bailey answered every pull of Scott's hand with a thrust of his own even though it seemed like he was going so fast and his heart was trying to catch up. Then, when he didn't think his body could go for any more, the tension crashed and the pleasure of release spurted out to coat the brick wall with thick, white splatters. It took a minute for his body to stop heaving and contracting. His body felt spent and empty when he was done and working on catching his breath.

"Step closer to the wall." Scott was still in officer mode even though he sounded like he'd run to chase down a perpetrator for a couple of miles. "Give me your left hand."

Bailey did as he said, but as his mind cleared he could hear more noises around them. He didn't think they were close, but he wasn't sure he'd been that quiet. Scott removed the handcuff he'd placed on one wrist and, with the scraping of his hands on the bricks and the hand around his cock, he'd forgotten all about that piece of hardware.

"Fix yourself, Bailey, and let's go."

He put himself together and shook his head. "I'm really not drunk, Scott. I can drive myself home. Plus, you never found my keys." Bailey pulled them out of his pocket and dangled them in front of Scott before the man snatched them and put them in his pocket.

"We both work here tomorrow night. I'll drive you back and you can get your car then." Scott seemed to inspect Bailey to make sure everything was back in order like he was going to walk through the parking lot with his cock out. If he did, he didn't think anyone would care. Scott then looked around the alleyway like he was expecting trouble.

"What's your deal?" Bailey asked as he followed Scott to his car.

"Just keeping my eyes on our surroundings. We've had some trouble with people who aren't the friendliest to gay men and get their jollies giving us a hard time on a good day, but trying to do physical harm on bad ones." Scott clicked his key fob that unlocked both of the doors and got in.

Bailey hadn't even thought of anything like that. He knew there were a good number of people who didn't appreciate anything other than heterosexuality, but until this moment he'd not considered himself a part of the homosexual community.

"I can see that this part of being interested in men hadn't really crossed your mind." Scott started the car.

"It really hadn't. I didn't mean to put us in harm's way. If I would have thought that through I would have made you use your officer Scotty voice on me at home. I just found this place earlier and when you came to collect me from my spot in the bar I thought nothing of using it."

"It's fine. All's well that ends well, right?"

Bailey watched the light from the passing street lights cross Scott's face. He wasn't sure if he could be this nonchalant about violence that loomed around the bar for no other reason than the jerks on the outside didn't like the sexual preferences of the men inside. "There has to be a way to protect people from that kind of small-minded prejudice."

"We try our best. Security inside and out...people keeping their ears and eyes open. The haters have been around for a long time and if there is a way to protect people from them completely, we've yet to find it." Scott looked briefly over to Bailey. "Not having sex outside the building so they can be caught unaware is a start."

"Um, I was just figuring that out. You could have stopped me at any time, though." Bailey was not going to feel bad about the hot situation that occurred outside, but now that he had more knowledge he wouldn't make the same mistake again, because he understood why that might not be a good idea.

Scott shook his head, but he had a small smile on his face. "So how was your date?"

Bailey smiled at Scott's tone because it was one he'd heard a million times from him. Not now, but in their distant past. Each and every time he'd done something with Honey without him, Scott would try to casually ask about it. "Beautiful woman, nice face, well put together...Ollie went out of his way to find this one. She was charming and attractive."

"Hmmm." Scott kept his eyes on the road, but his hands tightened on the steering wheel. He remembered this response as well and knew that if he didn't say another thing that would be the end of the conversation.

"She was pretty great and the food was delicious, but I left early and headed over to The Male Box." Bailey couldn't help but to study Scott as he took in all the information.

"When is your next date?"

"You ask a lot of questions for a guy who pushes me into a date with one hand, but jacks me off, and comes in his pants as he humps me in an alleyway in the other." Bailey wasn't sure why being with Scott was difficult for the man as he would have thought it would be something he would have been pleased with but each step was like walking through quicksand. He never knew what he'd do to make Scott disappear. It was worse than walking on egg shells and he was so sick of it.

"Yeah, I know. I'm not making my position clear."

"Not in the least, but I'm hoping that this excursion into the night to interrupt my time with the sweet assed dancer is going to end with more clarity than I have now." Bailey turned in time to see them turning up to Scott's mountain and he held on to the handle above the door. The look on Scott's face was of determination and he knew that this drive was a lot to maneuver the man had been doing this at least once a day for a few years and it shouldn't have taken this much concentration, but he gave the man a bit of time to get his thoughts together. They'd made it up the hill and Scott turned off the car, but he still didn't say anything. "Alright, dude. I'm going to bed."

"Wait." Scott put his hand on Bailey's chest like he was trying to keep him in the seat.

Bailey looked over and was glad that the man had put in sensor lights that turned on as soon as you got close to the house because he could see Scott's face clearly. It was clear there was a lot going on inside his head. "Yeah?"

"When did you meet Eric?"

Bailey took a deep breath because the dancer who'd befriended him in the bar wasn't what he wanted to talk about but he didn't want the conversation to end. "I met him tonight. He said the guys had told him I'd be working there soon and he wanted to introduce himself."

"He just walked up to you and said that? Then what happened?" Scott was still looking forward. It was like the man was talking to him on the telephone for as much as he looked at him. On the other hand, Bailey couldn't keep his gaze off Scott.

"Why? I'm sure he does that every day with a different person. It's the nature of the bar." Bailey just wanted a shower and to go to sleep. He had therapy with Honey in the morning and she kicked his ass enough when he was rested, but tomorrow would be more difficult than usual.

"You're right. That is the nature of most of the people in that bar, but Eric is a bit different. He doesn't mix with the staff or the customers on any level except to accept tips."

"Well, I don't know about that. He came over, introduced himself and then started a drinking game to figure out my name. When he guessed wrong, he'd drink and when I guessed something about him based on looks and was wrong, I drank. Good thing you showed up neither of us are good at guessing." Bailey smiled, thinking of the attractive man who'd kept coming back after his sets.

"So you liked Eric?" Scott's voice was quiet and so flat it almost didn't sound like Scott. Bailey knew all about this mood because he'd seen it so often before he'd left and maybe deep down he'd always known that the boy was into him. It was possible that he liked it then as well as he did now, but he hadn't been willing to look into it at that time.

"I did like him. Very much. He was fun, witty, attractive...*and*...He was into me." Bailey opened up the car door and got out before turning to lean back down into the car. "But he's no you."

Chapter 14

"HE'S NO YOU."

The words ran through Scott's head just as softly as they were when they were uttered. Bailey had closed the car door and headed into the house without him. He was going to have to do something. Shit or get off the pot, as his father would say. Scott got out of the car, walked to the house and opened the door, but Bailey was nowhere to be found. He did hear the shower though. He walked toward the sound praying that the part of him that could come up with language that communicated what he really meant would come back at this time and help him with Bailey but it was as it had been...silent.

Bailey sang in the shower like he hadn't a care in the world and it was true the man probably didn't. He was out of the military and working on his next stage of what to do with his life, he was in his hometown, had a bit of money saved up and people liked him. It was Scott who felt like he had the weight of the world on his shoulders. He had been given his teenaged fantasy come true in the form of his ultimate crush living in his home and the man actually wanting some form of physical attention from him. If it weren't for the promise he'd made his brother about doing anything to drive Bailey away again and fear that this experiment the man was having during his 'what's life all about' phase would kill him when it was over and he actually went back to anything that didn't include him in the co-star role he'd just roll with the punches. Scott stopped at that thought. *Was he crazy?* He was going to live a life regretting not just rolling with the punches with Bailey, if he didn't. The decision was made.

Scott knocked on the bathroom door after the water had turned off and after a minute or so the door opened and revealed Bailey with only a white towel he'd wrapped around his hips.

"Yes, Scott?" Bailey dried his hair and torso with another towel as he looked at himself in the mirror and Scott was transformed into the teen who used to marvel in the masculinity that was Bailey. He was tall, dark and the moderate amount of hair he had on his chest always made Scott want to rub his face on the man's chest and breathe in his scent. "Scott?"

Scott snapped out of the teen fantasy he'd been reliving and moved into the bathroom. "I was wrong to run from you...from this. As long as you want experience and I'm here...you've got it."

Bailey's eyes darkened and Scott wondered if that came from what he said or from what he meant. It didn't matter because either way Scott was excited by the prospect of having his favorite fantasy at his ready and available to him.

"Maybe then I'll be able to graduate past coming in my pants as well. Let me take a shower and then we can work more of this out," Scott said as he backed out of the door.

Bailey nodded and Scott turned to go to his room to get the stuff he needed to take a shower. When he returned the bathroom was empty. Scott turned on the water and it rained hot and hard onto his body, he remembered that Bailey hadn't really said anything while he was in the bathroom except to ask him what he wanted in the beginning, but Bailey was a big boy and if he had a problem with everything he'd tell him, of that he was pretty sure. Scott was soaped up and ready to rinse for the second time when he heard the bathroom door open and then he was standing face to face with a now naked Bailey. Whatever he'd imagined and what he'd actually seen had nothing on actually looking at this tall, lean, buffed out man in his bathroom with the lights on and desire in his eyes.

"I thought you might like some help." Bailey looked at Scott for confirmation and closed the frosted door behind him after Scott nodded. The roomy shower for one became a bit snug for two men, but Scott wasn't complaining one bit.

"A friend in need...is a friend indeed." Scott wanted to shake his head at how corny that was, but was rewarded with a laugh from Bailey.

"You always burst out with things like that when you don't know what to say." Bailey had reached for Scott and joined him as much as he could under the water spray pulling him close to him. "You can't tell me I make you nervous."

Scott shook his head, but he wasn't all together sure he wasn't lying. "Maybe a little."

Bailey leaned back a little to look into Scott's face. "Are you really?" The man sounded a bit shocked and Scott wondered if he knew how much he'd been into him before he left so many years ago.

Scott shrugged. "I'm just happy you're out of the military and here to have a bit of fun with me."

"So, officer, what do we do now?" Bailey was really just rubbing his hands all over Scott's body and it was relaxing and cool after the hot interaction they'd had in the alley.

"I have work in the morning and at night so after this shower, I say we talk for a bit and sort the rest out as we go."

Scott turned off the water then turned back to Bailey. The man was wet and naked, but they were both worn out. Hooking the larger man by the back of his neck Scott pulled him down for a kiss. He wanted it to be a thank you for not thinking Scott was an asshole and ending this situation before he could get his mind together, but the moans that came from Scott's throat made him turn this simple kiss into a more intricate one.

Bailey groaned back at him as he got into the kiss and pinched his fingers around the ring in his right nipple. "This doesn't bode well for getting some sleep soon."

Scott laughed and pushed Bailey back a little. "You're right." He got out of the shower and started drying off with a towel when the towel was taken and Bailey finished the job for him before walking out of the bathroom and into the room where Bailey slept. Scott followed him and watched him put on a pair of black boxer briefs.

"We don't have much time to sleep," Scott said as he watched Bailey in the mirror.

"No, we don't. You get up pretty early and it's really late now."

"Maybe I'll just sleep in here." Now Scott knew that this argument had no basis but he wasn't ready to admit that now that he'd made up his mind about letting go of this situation and allowing the Bailey cards to fall where they may, he didn't want to waste a single second of the time he could be spending with him.

Bailey stared at him like he was trying to figure him out, but in the end he pulled down the comforter and crawled into bed. "You are welcome in whatever bed I'm in at any time."

Scott turned off the light by the door and found the bed in the darkness. The same darkness that witnessed the broad smile that was plastered across his face. He laid down next to Bailey and took a deep breath in. Now that he was this far in what to do, he was unsure. Snuggle up with him? Maybe that was too much. Lay, like he was on the other side of the mattress? That wouldn't be bad since he still had his way of lying in bed with Bailey.

"You are thinking so loud it's disturbing me." Bailey pulled Scott into the warmth of his huge body and Scott relaxed into him. "That's so much better, isn't it?"

"If you say so," Scott replied cheekily. He was sexually satisfied, and happy, but Bailey talking to him in the dark room had Scott growing a half chub even as his exhausted body fought sleep.

Bailey moved his hand down to cup Scott's cock and balls casually. Like it was a ritual he'd done to himself, but now used Scott since he was in that space. He gave a soft squeeze that was more comforting than arousing but that chuckle was pure filthy. "I do say so."

Chapter 15

BAILEY WOKE UP IN HIS bed alone and the bright sun told him Honey would be here at any moment. He got up and noticed he had a text message.

Bailey,

You are a cover hog, but it doesn't matter because you give off body heat like a furnace. I'll be home around four. If you want, we can get something to eat before heading off to The Male Box. Let me know if you want me to pick something up. S.

Bailey stood smiling at his phone because he'd not been sure the carefree-ish attitude and the ability to stay with him for more than 20 minutes without looking like he was stalking the door was great. He went to the bathroom and put on his PT attire of sweatpants and a t shirt. The doorbell rang and Bailey was ready.

The workouts were getting easier and more manageable. Bailey was pleased with how Honey seemed to get what she needed from him in a way that wasn't nagging or irritating. She just moved him from one exercise to the next, but suddenly Bailey had questions about their past.

"Honey?"

"Hmm?" She was writing down something in the little book she brought out when he was training.

"Why did you leave me in high school?" Bailey really wanted the answer to the question that plagued him so much lately.

Honey put down the pad of paper and looked at him. "Why do you want to go over this now? That was so far in the past."

"I get that, but I didn't understand it then and I really don't understand it now. Here you are coming all the way up this mountain two to three times a week, for no payment, and we sit here acting like there wasn't a time you broke my heart so bad I left town." Bailey watched her as she fiddled with the pad of paper and her pen.

"That wasn't how it was, Bailey and you know it." Honey put the pen and paper down and stood up to walk toward the window.

"Really? That's how it seemed to me, so if it seemed like something else from your perspective, I'd love to hear it."

Honey wasn't one to fidget, but she was doing it now. "Do you like Scott?"

"What does that have to do with anything?" Bailey stopped his work out to concentrate on her.

"We went to his 18th birthday together," Honey said and then stopped. "Well, we were supposed to go together, but then I offered to help put things together before people got there for the party."

Bailey didn't really remember the details, but vaguely remembers her not being with him when he arrived. *"Okay."*

"I saw you from the time you got out of your car. I was always so proud to have a boyfriend like you. Everyone always looked at me with wonder." Honey had a smile on her face as she took this solo trip down memory lane. She wasn't really looking at Bailey. It was like she was telling him a story about someone else. "I was the geeky preacher's kid that never got into any trouble and wasn't allowed to wear the newest fashions or make-up like everyone else, but somehow I ended up with the cutest boy in school who was such a faithful boyfriend girls asked me for advice."

Bailey had no idea where she was going, but he'd wanted to know what had spurred their sudden break up and it appeared that now she was willing to talk about it.

"I'd actually give the girls what they wanted in terms of advice, but little did I know I really didn't have any to give." Honey finished and then covered her face with her hands. Bailey could see she was becoming upset while telling her story, but he wasn't understanding where she was going.

"I'm trying to follow you and this story, Honey, but I don't see where this is the answer to my question. Unless you're saying you left me because you didn't think you gave good advice." Bailey was puzzled when Honey finally did look at him she seemed so sad. "How can you sit there and look sad when you're the one who left me? You did it without notice or explanation and the whole community was pissed that I'd done something to you they damn near throttled me with words every time they saw me."

"Back to the birthday party," she continued, sitting on the chair closest to Bailey, Honey took a deep breath, sat up straight like she was readying herself and looked into his eyes. "You got out of your car and walked over to the pool where everyone was but you stopped before you turned the corner where everyone would see you." Honey spoke like she wanted him to remember what had happened and he tried to recall that day. Scott's 18th birthday party.

He remembered the day, but he didn't remember doing anything that would have pissed Honey off so bad she'd be so done with him she wouldn't speak another word for years.

"Before you got to the place where everyone could see you, Scott got out of the pool and your eyes fixed on him." Honey picked up her glass of water and drank it down like she needed it to get through the telling of this tale.

"You left me because I watched Scott get out of the pool?" Bailey was hoping for more than this because it didn't make any sense.

"The look of desire I saw on your face looking at Scott was more than I'd ever seen you have. It was bigger than the desire you had for Albert's Chocolate chip ice cream, a win for your team, or anything you'd ever had for me."

There was silence between them and he struggled to figure out what to say about that.

"You liked Scott and it brought out all the times I'd done things I thought you'd like and desire but it wasn't there. I remember trying to make out with you or go further than making out but you weren't interested. You'd say something about keeping me pure and respecting me too much, but the honest fact was that you weren't into me." Honey looked away in the end and Bailey didn't know what to say.

He remembered that day clearly now, he'd walked up to the pool and could hear all the people who were there at the party, but he'd only had eyes for the wet birthday boy who'd emerged from the water like a wet dream. He'd been startled by the strength of his desire as well, but he'd thought that was a private moment.

"I'm not asking you to dispute or explain what was going on in your head when you saw Scott, but I was full on, green eyed fury."

"You couldn't have talked to me about it?" Bailey didn't even know why he was trying with this, but he'd thought about this a lot over the years

"Bailey. You'd never have wanted to hurt my feelings and you'd have smoothed it over with me if I asked, but I know what I saw. You'd never looked at me like that. It was hot and sexy and it wasn't for me."

"You and Scott were friends you could have asked him if you thought something was going on between us." Bailey put down his exercise bands because he was getting a workout just listening to this conversation.

Honey moved closer to Bailey and put her hand on his arm. "I never thought you were cheating on me or doing something wrong. I just knew you weren't into me like I thought you were. All those times I thought you were just being a gentleman and didn't want to sully my reputation or my virtue it was a lie. You weren't into me like that."

Bailey could barely look at her. "I was a true asshole to you, Honey and until today I didn't really know it. I didn't have the kind of feelings you had for me, but I loved you. I thought we'd be together forever and I was planning to marry you."

"I know you loved me, Bailey, but did you want me?"

"I was a fool." Bailey stood up and wanted to get away from Honey. How did he not know what a jerk he was to her? He'd actually been upset that she left him, but looking back how could she have stayed?

"That was a long time ago and we're friends again now." Honey hugged him and Bailey hugged her back. Thankful to know what really happened and shocked that she'd seen something that he'd been running from for the last 8 years, but something came to him.

"Did you talk to Scott about any of this?" Bailey looked into her face and the pink tint on her cheeks told the story better and quicker than she ever would.

"I may have said something to him about you a few days after we split. I asked him to take care of you. I knew that he'd already been by your side since we'd split up and I knew Ollie was out of town so he wouldn't be able to help." Honey went back to hugging him. "You have always been the best hugger."

Bailey pushed her back a little and looked down into her face. "What did you say to Scott?"

"I asked him to make sure you were alright and I told him I thought you may have some feelings for him." Honey backed up from him a little more and he wondered what his face must look like. That night in the back of his truck looking at the stars with Scott, he wondered what had gotten into him that he would crawl on top of him and kiss him like that. He'd tried to talk himself into thinking it was just because the guy was trying to comfort him. Bailey had tried to temper his own response to being so red hot and ready for the smaller man because he'd not jerked off in a while or because he was so sad being dumped any upgrade in feelings worked, but it wasn't that. He'd always known it wasn't that. He'd liked the gruff feel of a man on top of him and the hard rough kiss that accompanied it. The two of them had rubbed their cocks together like they were trying to start a fire with kindling and when Bailey had come it had been more explosive than he'd ever come in his life. It wasn't until the cum had dried in his shorts and he realized how relaxed and exhilarated he got from holding Scott in his arms. "Bailey?"

"Yeah." He startled out of his sexy flashback and tried to bring himself to the matter at hand. "I'm just thinking."

"What are you thinking about?" Honey looked worried.

"A lot of things, but really how I wish you'd have talked to me sooner. Things work out the way they do and everything supposedly happens for a reason, but there has been so much time wasted." Bailey wondered if anything would have changed if she confronted him about this earlier but figured it probably wouldn't have. He'd been terrified at the time of looking into his feelings and if she'd have mentioned it, he'd have shoved it so far back in his closet he'd have married Honey and had kids by now.

"Time wasted for what?" Honey asked with her eyes squinted. "I'm asking because the look of lust I witnessed on your face toward Scott when he turned 18 is only a spark compared to how you look at him now."

Bailey turned toward Honey quickly and was surprised by the grin on her face.

"I've always been able to read you when it came to other people. It was reading how you felt toward me that was the issue. I guess it really wasn't though, because you just weren't that into me."

"Things happened, after you broke up with me and apparently spoke to Scott, that I wasn't prepared to handle at the time, but I've thought about how to make heads and tails out of what happened then." Bailey walked over to Honey. "I'd never have done what I did to you on purpose. Yes, I liked you because you weren't pushy with sex, but you were also amazing to bounce ideas off of and you were an expert bowler."

Honey smacked him playfully in the arm.

"Seriously." Bailey caught her chin between his fingers and steadied her face toward his so she could pay attention to him. "You meant so much to me that I really was heartbroken when you dumped me. I was so confused, but listening to you now I was confused about a lot of things. I want to thank you for pushing me off the cliff instead of letting me stay comfortable in untruths."

"What are friends for?" Honey broke out of his chin grasp and hugged him right when Scott walked in with bags. The man walked in with a smile on his face, but it fell a bit when he saw the two of them hugging in the middle of the room.

"Hey Scott, what did you bring home?" Bailey held on to Honey's hand and walked behind Scott to the kitchen.

"Just some General Tso's Chicken and a few egg rolls. If you haven't figured out that most delivery food places don't deliver up here on the mountain." Scott set out two plates and took all the food out of the bags.

"Honey, are you going to stay and eat with us?" Bailey asked ushering her to the table.

"No. I have to get to my next appointment."

"I was going to run too." Scott was finishing up getting the table set up and then he picked up a few things and he was ready to go.

Bailey watched the two of them scramble to get to the door. "Wait."

The both of them turned around.

"What the hell is this? I feel like both of you are running away from me...do I smell?" Bailey was trying to be casual and funny but he felt as if something was going on.

Honey rushed over to Scott and gave him a kiss on the cheek. "You tell him." Then she moved to Bailey and gave him a hug. "I really do have to run. I have other clients."

Bailey watched Scott track Honey around the room and he didn't stop looking at the door, she walked out of until the door closed.

"Want to tell me what that was about?" Bailey moved to reach for Scott and pulled him closer to him.

"Not really, but I guess since she put it all out there and then left I'll have to fill you in." Scott gave Bailey a quick kiss and then gave his butt a quick smack. "It will have to be over lunch though, because I knew I'd only have time to eat when I brought this before I had to go back to work."

They moved to the table and made their plates, but it didn't seem like Scott was in a rush to tell him what had just gone on between his two friends.

"I'm not going to let you leave until you tell me and I'm sure I'm going to have follow up questions so the sooner you start, the sooner we finish." Bailey was trying to keep his mind off Scott in his uniform and what he really wanted to do with him in it.

"Back in the day when we were all friends there were times you were so oblivious to the petty rivalry that went on daily between Honey and I." Scott stopped and took a bit of his food.

"What rivalry?" Bailey shoveled food into his mouth to force himself not to ask questions until Scott was done, but apparently it wasn't working.

"Exactly my point. Honey and I did so many things to compete for your attention. I was always along on your time together and I think she kind of hated it but we were friends too.

It was a love/hate relationship, but it grew to be more hate after you two broke up." Scott took another bite of his food and a drink. Bailey wanted to know more, but he didn't say anything. "We both blamed each other for you leaving and Ollie blamed both of us. It was a bad scene."

"In these competitions what would you do? How did you determine who won? What did you get?" Bailey scooped a bit more food onto his plate wondering how he didn't notice this.

Scott laughed. "Are you kidding? Everything was a competition. If you wanted to eat and I suggested something so would Honey. Whoever's idea you chose would win. What did we win? Nothing really, but we were playing for your time and affection. I'd have never let me stay around if I were Honey but you didn't mind it so I guess she didn't either."

"So you're telling me that since you were like that then you, what, agreed not to do it again?" Bailey thought he was catching on.

"When we heard you were coming back we said that we wouldn't let you get into the way of our friendship and we wouldn't revert to our high school selves." Scott chuckled to himself a bit more. "I was planning on staying away from you, so it wasn't going to be a problem for me. It was Ollie that threw a big wrench in that plan."

"What?" Bailey frowned at Scott.

Scott looked at his watch. "Wow! Look at the time. I've got to go. I'll be back in a couple hours and we can head back to the bar."

"Don't think I'll forget what I was going to ask about Ollie before you suddenly had to go."

Scott bent over and kissed Bailey softly on his mouth and trailed biting kisses from there to the soft skin below his ear. "I'm sure you have more questions and I'll answer as many of them as I can."

"Were some of them classified?" Bailey smirked, thinking of how Scott talked about answering some of the questions.

"They feel that way." Scott gave him one last quick peck before straightening up and turning to walk out. "Sorry I can't help clean up. I'll cook and clean next time."

Bailey watched Scott walk out and didn't look away from the door the man walked out of until he heard the door close. Was he really that unobservant back in the day? He'd not known he was that interested in Scott until the man made a move on him but maybe that wasn't the case. Bailey stood up and cleaned the table before taking a nap. It was like he was learning about a past he was involved in but not really a part of...is that possible? Apparently, it was.

Cleaning the table and thinking about other things that had been said that he just let slide he remembered Ollie's almost anger at Honey. He knew the man was mad about the break up, but that was so long ago he couldn't still be mad about that, but he decided to call him and find out.

He pulled out his phone and pressed the button assigned to his best friend...number two.

"Hey, Bailey. What's up? I thought I'd hear from you after you left from the date I set up. I'm sorry if she wasn't your type, but I have lots of other friends," Ollie said without waiting for a greeting of any kind.

"It's no big deal. I thought Candy was great, but it's not really what I'm into right now." Bailey rushed to the next part because he really didn't want to get into that with Ollie right at this point. "Actually, I'm calling with some questions for you."

"Oh, yeah? You know I'm an open book."

Bailey could hear papers ruffling in the background. "Is this a good time for you? I know people have regular jobs during regular hours, but as of yet, I'm not one of them."

"Nah. What I'm doing I can talk and do it. What's up?"

"Why are you so mad at Honey?" Bailey waited so long for an answer, he wondered if the disconnection was bad, but he could swear that he could hear Ollie on the other line. "Ollie?"

"Why are you asking about her? Please don't say you two are getting back together."

"That's not where I was going with the question, but I'm just thinking back to your attitude when you saw her the other day and I wondered what she'd done to you." Bailey finished cleaning up the kitchen and went to sit on the comfy couch preparing to hear whatever was coming next.

"She's a trouble maker and she went out of her way to stir the pot. Honey is the reason you left."

Bailey had a choice to make but he didn't have all the pieces to do so. Things were way too new with Scott to hit him with the fact he and his best friend's baby brother were exploring each other sexually and he didn't really want to tell him the real reason why he left.

"There are things you don't know about, Ollie, and I'm not sure I want to go into them, but Honey isn't the reason I left."

"That's what you think," Ollie spat, clearly disgusted with any and all talks about Honey.

"No. That's what I know."

"Bailey. You are my very best friend and you are good at so many things, but being aware of the emotions of people around you isn't your strong suit... at least it wasn't at that time." Ollie softened his voice like he was speaking to someone who needed soothing. He had been a selfish man in the past who only saw what he obviously wanted to see. Damn, he hoped he'd changed.

"So tell me what I'm missing."

"Oh...you want to hear about it?" Ollie said and the question in his voice made him wonder what he would have said before.

"Of course I want to hear about it. I care about all of you and I feel like things were happening around me that I wasn't aware of and I left here thinking I was saving myself but I didn't realize I was damaging so many others."

"What you're missing is that my brother has had a thing for you for years and you never knew about it. He followed you everywhere. We both stuck up for him with the bullies when he was younger and I thought that he just felt safer around you but it was more than that."

"I knew he liked me Ollie. Damn, I wasn't that clueless."

"You were clueless to how much your girlfriend hated it. One thing I never understood is why she seemed to genuinely like Scott."

Bailey stood up and paced the room. The energy he had inside was making him restless. "So you don't like Honey, because she let Scott stay around? Ollie, I don't understand what you're trying to say. I need you to be a bit clearer. Spell it out for me."

"Honey broke up with you for reasons I will never know, but then she came at Scott with all this shit about you being in-

THERE GOES MY BAILEY 133

to him. He came on to you and you left like a thief in the night. She started the shit rolling and then I come home from camp and my best friend is gone with only a shitty letter that doesn't say much and plans we'd had since we were kids discarded like trash." Ollie was breathing like he'd been walking on the treadmill on five while he talked and Bailey couldn't have felt more like a heel if he tried.

"So you talked to Scott about this?"

"I had quite a few choice words for both of them and I'm not going into what they were. Let's just say Scott was more willing to own up to his part in this and of course he's my brother so I would have to eventually forgive him."

Bailey wanted to say so much more, but he didn't have enough of the story to do so. "Well, I'm glad you and your brother are good, but I wish you'd let go of whatever anger you had at Honey. It was a long time ago, man."

Ollie took a deep breath in and Bailey knew he was trying to pull himself together.

"I know, but I see her and see red."

"I get it, but maybe we all need a reset. I'm home now and I'm not going anywhere anytime soon so think about letting this go." Bailey walked up the stairs to his bedroom and sat on the bed. He'd been curled up with Scott right here in this bed, but they hadn't slept long enough to savor each other. Laying down in the spot where Scott was, he could almost smell him and it was comforting and arousing at the same time. "Look, I got to get some sleep. I'm going to be a bartender where Scott works so I'm going to be up late."

"The Male Box?" Ollie asked.

"Yep, Scott knows the owner and—"

"Mark, right?"

"Right." Bailey was shocked he knew that, but then maybe he'd met him when Scott was together with him. He decided he wasn't going to get upset about that. Bailey was asking people to let bygones be bygones so he had his nerve getting upset about Scott's past relationships. Especially since what they had going on now wasn't really a relationship...it wasn't even a trial. It was an experience. "So I'll talk to you later."

"Alright, Bailey. I'll see you soon."

Hanging up the phone he lay breathing in the fresh and clean aroma of Scott and thinking. *What the fuck am I getting myself into?* If thinking that his time with Scott meant less than nothing was causing that twisting in his chest, he may need to rethink what he was willing to accept from him, but for now... sleep.

Chapter 16

SCOTT HAD NEVER BEEN happier to have an excuse not to talk to Bailey. It seemed he'd had a busy day speaking to Honey, Ollie and himself. The questions in his eyes before they got on the road to head to work almost lit him up from the inside. Scott had only gotten a few hours of sleep the night before and he'd had to get up and work a full eight hour shift that turned into ten hours with the domestic dispute that hit them right before quitting time. Now he was on his way to his second job and there was no way he would have been able to handle the questions he undoubtedly had with the limited brain power he had available. He slept on the way to work and let Bailey drive.

Now he was stuck by the door, watching the wildly popular new bartender get swarmed with people looking for drinks or giving offers to suck him off on his break. Scott knew how it was to be new meat to a pack of hungry men, and he knew how appealing Bailey was. The man could get experience anywhere. Scott wondered if Bailey knew that, then he wondered if he'd want something different if he could have something different. It wasn't like that was off the table for either of them.

"How's it going tonight?" Mark must have come from the other way, but his ability to sneak up on him told Scott that his mind definitely wasn't on security tonight.

"Pretty good. What's up with you?" Scott felt bad just standing here with Mark, because they'd talked almost every day for years, even if it was just a hello text, but with Bailey around he'd pretty much given up everything but things that had to do with Bailey.

"Just living life." Mark was looking around and Scott wondered what he was getting ready to say. Mark was no shuffler. This man got right to the point.

"How are you and Bailey doing?"

"There is no me and Bailey. We are two people who live in the same house." Scott's gaze caught on Mark's weird smirk. "What?"

"I'm just wondering how long you took to come up with that and if you really believe that?" Mark was back to his confident and maddening self. It was hard not to smile, remembering how many times this man had pulled him out of the doldrums and usually with a swift verbal kick in the pants.

"I believe in what I'm saying, Mark."

"Oh good. I just wanted you to know that Eric has plans for your Bailey and they sound pretty hot, but if you don't care, then I guess I don't need to tell you about them." Mark tipped his head toward the bar and Scott looked over in time to see Eric and Bailey with their heads together like they were again telling secrets to each other.

"No you don't. This is a gay bar and people come here to get information about themselves and about what they like. I'm not concerned about what Bailey is doing or getting into. He's a grown man and can make his own decisions." Scott was surprised he could come up with that much bullshit at one time but apparently he was pretty good at it. Even Mark looked convinced. The truth was he didn't even know why he was trying to keep it from Mark but he wasn't ready to let anyone in their little bubble, but by the look of Bailey with Eric the bubble had burst...or it was about to.

"Well, good for you." Mark started to walk off, then turned back around. "Your acting skills are getting better, pet, but I don't believe that shit for a minute."

Scott just smiled at him. It was kind of nice having someone know who you really were and be there to support you whether they agreed with what you were doing and saying.

Bailey and Eric had walked off in the direction of the bathrooms and Scott knew all about what happened in those rooms, but he wasn't going to run after Bailey like he had as a teen. Those days were over and if the man wanted to get sucked off in the bathroom of the bar so be it. It had happened to him in his early years of being wild and acting out so it's an experience that he probably needs to go through. The minutes ticked away and so did Scott's good mood. Was it possible to send a message telepathically? Scott stared at the last place Bailey had been seen every few minutes with thoughts of what was probably happening going through his mind. It wasn't supposed to matter. In theory, he knew this in his mind, but the cells that controlled jealousy didn't get the memo.

"I brought you a water."

Scott was so busy looking at where he thought Bailey had gone, he'd missed that he'd somehow doubled back and was now beside him. He accepted the beverage and cracked open the top before drinking most of it down. "Thank you."

"No problem. I'm on break so I thought I'd come over and say hello." Bailey stopped like he wanted to say something and Scott waited patiently for him to get to what he wanted to say. "Look, I'm not good at this with women and I seem to be even worse with men so I'm just going to say what I want to say and if it lacks finesse, just know that's the way I am."

Scott nodded and took another swig of his water.

"I know you said we are to be getting experience and I'm all for that, but I don't think I'm the run out and get experience type of dude." Bailey sat on the tall stool that was given to the security team to rest so they wouldn't wear out, but still look badass because the black leather, silver studded, high back stool was pretty wicked.

"Maybe you're not giving yourself enough time." Scott had no idea why such bullshit came running out of his mouth...well, maybe he did. He and his brother were close, they always had been there for each other no matter what...until Scott had fucked up and Ollie's best friend left. It was months before the man would be around him of his own accord and more months after that before they got close to the place of friendship they'd lived all their lives. He'd promised his brother, he'd never do anything to compromise Bailey being there and he'd never doubted that he would keep his word to Ollie, but it had been easier to keep when Bailey was nowhere to be found.

Bailey reached out and pulled Scott into the space between his legs. "I've given myself lots of time. I'm not a child, Scott. I know what I like and I know who I want. If you aren't available or not willing let me know, but other than that, I want you. You alone, you under me, you over me, you around me, you through me. I want you in all the ways I can have you." Bailey pulled him in closer with a hand on the back of his neck and placed several sweet warm kiss on his mouth.

Scott wondered briefly who was watching this amazing moment he was receiving while he was at work. It wasn't the rough and tumble kisses they usually shared. This one was sweet and hot. For an instant Scott wondered if people were questioning what was going on but first it was none of their business and next who the fuck cared. He was kissing Harold Fucking Bailey.

The kiss broke and Bailey pushed Scott lightly away and frowned at him like a thought crossed his mind that he didn't like. "I have a new rule. Don't kiss anytime the other person can see you."

Scott tried to be upset about that, but he was happy it was something he'd thought about, but he wasn't going to fess up to it. "What made you come up with that?"

"I can see you over here just as clearly as you can see me at the bar. Mark has been circling you all night and then I watched him make his way over here. I pleaded with whoever above that is listening to help him not give you a kiss when I can see it. It's been the worst part of my night. Beside that I think I'm going to like this job and I surely should have brought my piggy bank."

Scott was more than pleased to talk to Bailey without thinking he's going to ask questions he didn't want to answer. "It's not over, the big hitters come around a few hours before closing."

"I'm guessing that's the booty call pick up time?" Bailey smiled and Scott's breath caught. Damn, if he wasn't falling back in time to his teen crush years. Only this time it seemed like his feelings were reciprocated.

"You are correct."

"Have you ever partaken with customers? It seems like the place to hook up if you were in the right mindset." Bailey searched Scott's face like he was looking for answers.

"There was a time when I did have fun here, but most of these people are regulars and I'm not into commitment in general." Scott could honestly say that was the true reason he didn't play here, but with Bailey looking like he wanted more answers to that he didn't know if that was true now... in this moment... with Bailey. Would he do commitment with his lifelong crush? Abso-fucking-lutely, but he'd been out here for years and Bailey was just starting. Watching him learn the ropes and find out more about his sexuality would be difficult, but while he was still interested in Scott. He'd help Bailey out as much as possible.

Jax, who was one of the cooks, was out from the back. Mark always liked to make sure he had at least one break at night and if Jax was there he was the one who usually relieved him from his duties.

"Hey, dude. You ready to take a break? I made Stromboli for you if you're hungry."

"Thanks, Jax," Scott gave the man a playful punch on the arm and the large gruff biker looking man smiled shyly.

"Anytime, man." Jax nodded at Bailey with a weird look on his face so Scott looked to see what would be causing that.

"My name is Bailey. I'm the newest bartender."

Scott didn't think he'd ever seen this demeanor on his laid back, care free friend. It would be a lie if he said he didn't notice the green eyed monster. He recognized that emotion well, as it was a close companion back in the day. Hell, who was he kidding, he felt a twinge of it every time he was around Bailey.

THERE GOES MY BAILEY   141

"Jax." The man stuck out his hand and Bailey shook it. "I work in the kitchen and give Scott a break when he needs one."

Bailey nodded, but looked between the two men. "Nice to meet you."

"Same here."

Scott felt like déjà vu because he'd felt the same way when this micro confrontation was between Mark and Bailey. Weirdly aroused.

"Come on, Bailey. I wanted to show you something and then we can eat the deliciousness that Jax made."

Bailey followed behind Scott he could feel it. Since he'd been dreading Bailey getting his first bar blow he figured he may as well give it to him. At least he'll remember it the next time it happens with someone else. Shit...even thinking that still felt like a physical punch.

They made into the bathroom and there weren't that many people in there. Just a couple of guys hanging around the back stalls. Scott opened the larger one and stepped inside.

Bailey crossed his arms in front of his chest and stood with his legs shoulder width apart. "What's this?"

"A rite of passage."

"Getting sucked off in a bathroom is a rite of passage?" Bailey sounded grumpy. He couldn't still be salty about Jax could he?

"Yes, are you going to turn it down?" Scott met Bailey in the center and unbuckled his belt.

"Maybe I've done this already," Bailey said, and Scott froze.

The man never said he'd not done anything, maybe—

"I haven't. I just wanted to see your face when I asked the question." Bailey smiled at him and he wondered what game he was playing. It also made him wonder if he'd had any experience. He thought about the conversations they'd had up to this point and he didn't remember hearing anything like that.

Scott was thrown off guard by the way Bailey caressed his face, cupped his chin and brought him in for a soft kiss before putting his hand on his head while he lowered himself to the floor.

This was going to be fast and dirty just like it was supposed to be inside a bathroom stall in a bar. Scott quickly undid the buttons and withdrew the thick cock that he'd seen outlined in his youth and now. A month ago if someone would have told him all this would be happening to him he wouldn't have believed it.

"Seeing you on your knees for me is a treat I've always wanted. I'm going to admit I've been worked up all day thinking about last night so this may not last as long as you think it will." Bailey was looking down on Scott and although sucking cock was one of his favorite things to do, it didn't actually make him hard until it was his turn to have something done to him. Not this time. Just having Bailey's eyes on him was turning him on more than it should but he refused to spend the rest of this night with cum in his pants. That's for damn sure.

Scott caught Bailey's large cock at its base and stroked it to the tip. The gasp that came from above him encouraged him to go all in. The sights, sounds, smells and tastes that came from cock were different with each and every one he'd ever been with but he didn't remember being so interested in remembering each detail as he was with this one. He studied it while he stroked and watched for what Bailey liked the best. It was difficult to take his attention off the face he lov...liked so much, but he wanted to experience it all so he moved his attention to the organ he was about to pleasure. The fat mushroomed head was a darker pink than the shaft and the whole thing was brighter than it had just been when he started. Scott opened his mouth and wrapped his lips just around the head and almost moaned at the taste. That noise was overpowered as Bailey hissed long and slow before grabbing Scott's head.

He waited just a few seconds to see if Bailey was going to move him in the tempo that he wanted, but he seemed content to just hold on to him while he sucked on his cock's tip. He stayed here for a bit and just enjoyed sliding the sensitized flesh in and out of his mouth. When he opened his mouth a little more, he looked up to see Bailey looking at him in a way he'd always dreamed of and Scott lowered his eyes afraid of what Bailey would see reflected back at him. Scott took a bit more into his mouth moving further down, drawing more of his warm flesh inside him. This was such a fucking bad idea. Scott wanted nothing more than to explore Bailey's body all day and here they were stuck at work.

"Yes, Scott, just like that. Just like that." Bailey had his bottom lip between his teeth when Scott took a chance and looked up. The man's hips were making small circles cluing Scott to the fact that he was trying to hold back...but that's not what bathroom blow jobs were about. They were about letting loose, heightened sensations and blowing your wad in a release that felt so good you were willing to find out who was in the bathroom to do it again. Scott was going to have to get out of his own head if he was going to shake Bailey up enough to see why this was a rite of passage.

Scott loved that just Bailey's cock and balls were outside his clothes. He'd staged him just like he wanted him like he needed more things to turn him on about this situation. There was something so dirty and inhibited about the look, but on this man it was making him come undone. Opening wide Scott took as much of Bailey's cock as he could as he used his hand to extend the reach of pleasure he was able to give.

The low growl that came from above made Scott look up to see Bailey's eyes closed as he started pumping his hips in earnest. *Yes!*

"Fuck, Scott. Don't stop, baby, please don't stop."

Scott doubled up his efforts to keep up with the deep thrusts of his partner until Bailey froze for a few seconds.

"I'm gonna come." Bailey tried to move away from Scott's hungry mouth, but there was no way in hell he was going to let him blow this on the bathroom floor. He was still pissed the wall in the alley got a piece of Bailey. *"Fuuuccck."* The growl rumbled against the walls of the bathroom and seemed to echo.

Scott tried to get every drop, but it was difficult, because the man's loads were huge but this one was massive. Bailey's abs flexed and contracted in quick bursts from the aftermath of such a huge orgasm and Scott was very proud of himself.

Being dragged up to his feet and pushed against the wall was new for Scott. He wasn't the biggest man, but he was always the top. They may have touched on the topic, but it wasn't something he'd gotten into with Bailey yet. The way Bailey held on to Scott's face devouring his mouth, biting his lips and pulling him up on his tip toes made him feel desirable more than he thought it would.

Bailey moved one of his hands down to his pants and made quick work of his button fly jeans. He dropped to his knee and sucked Scotts cock into his mouth without preliminary touches and sucked him like he needed the fluid inside to live another day. Scott wished he could have told him to slow down, or give him a minute, but the intensity of the moment and the amazing sensation on his cock made his orgasm almost instantaneous. The howling sound that escaped Scott's mouth sounded like a wounded dog, but he couldn't have stopped it if he tried. He'd wanted Bailey to come undone, but it was him who was blown apart in that bathroom.

"You taste pretty good, Scotty."

Now it was his turn to get himself back together and it was hard to even fuss at him about the use of the name he hated so much. Bailey stood up and got himself back together and Scott did the same. Then they both stood against the stall walls staring at each other.

"We are going to have to eat quick if you're hungry. I'm sure our breaks are over," Bailey said, pushing off the wall and pulling Scott to him. "I'm sure your wannabe boyfriend will wrap it up to go."

"Jealous much?" Scott wanted to lighten the mood and knew that Bailey wouldn't ever cop to something so emotional as jealousy.

"Not typically, but lately...yes."

Scott was shocked when he turned his gaze to Bailey. "You aren't the Bailey I remember."

"Good. I hope I'm better than he was."

Chapter 17

IT HAD BEEN TWO WEEKS of fun, laughs and fucking. Well, no actual penetration, but for whatever reason it seemed like Scott was either saving that for something special or he wasn't that into it. It didn't matter since the two of them worked together, slept together and stayed together most of the time. There was no more of Scott running from him or looking like he was going to drown in guilt every time they'd had a sexual encounter so all was right in his world.

"Gimmie the regular." One of the customers that was here every day Bailey was here said.

"Sure thing. You want me to open up a tab?" Bailey knew the man did, but he asked him every time. Who knew maybe the answer would be different.

"That's a great idea." The man said that every time too, like it was a novel idea.

Bailey was settling in and he didn't remember being this content at any other point in his life.

"Give me what he's having."

Bailey turned to the familiar voice and found Ollie sitting on the stool in front of him. The smile that spread over his face was contagious and he moved around the bar to give him a big hug.

"What are you doing here?" Bailey made a drink with scotch and soda before passing the glass over to him.

"Well, when I talk to Scott it seems like the two of you are here most nights so if I want to see either of you, I guess this is the place to be." Ollie picked up his drink and took a swig.

THERE GOES MY BAILEY 147

Bailey shrugged. They'd been picking up a good number of hours, but they were home more than they were here. He wasn't sure why Scott was giving Ollie the impression they worked so much. "So you wanted to see us or did you have something special to say?"

"I do, but it looks like a few people are in need of a refill. I don't mind waiting. It'll be like the time you worked at the soda shop, I hung around there so much I should have gotten paid." Ollie looked around the bar like he was taking in the place and Bailey was getting the feeling something wasn't right. He tried to put his finger on it before he got back in front of Ollie, but he couldn't figure it out.

"Do you want another?" Bailey asked Ollie.

"Sure. Keep them coming."

Bailey turned to get another drink and Scott came around the corner looking like he was going to pull Bailey into a corner or a back room.

"Let me steal you away for a bit," Scott said in a low sexy voice. Although they'd been having fun finding new places to get frisky, he thought the man may want to know his brother was there.

"Say hello to your brother, and then you can take me where ever you want." Bailey went to lean down to give Scott a quick kiss and the man moved out of his arms so quickly it was hard to remember he'd been almost in his arms.

"Hey Ollie, what's up?" Scott's voice was tense as was his demeanor. Bailey moved up close to his back to get in Scott's space and to hear what Ollie was going to say. He made the drink and set it in front of Ollie before settling into Scott, who seemed to bristle a little.

"Not much. I was just telling Bailey since you guys are here practically every night I'm going to come and visit with you here. Looks like a lively place." Ollie smiled and took another look around the room.

"It doesn't bother you that you'll be sitting in a gay bar while you do it?" Bailey had to ask because it would bother him if he didn't get that question answered.

"Not at all. You're straight and comfortable here so I can be too."

"Well, I—" Bailey wanted to get this out in the open so bad, but there hadn't been a time and he didn't think Bailey wanted a lot of his business out in the open. He seemed to be a very private person when it came to his brother.

"Yeah, Bailey holds his own in here. They won't bother you unless you want it. Right, Bailey?" Scott looked up at him and he could see the pleading in his eyes and it fucking crushed his heart. So in the club they were okay, in the house they were okay, but now that he thought about it there was no time they were in public. Maybe Scott was embarrassed by him. He backed away from Scott, but nodded the answer to the question and went to make more drinks while the brothers talked.

Bailey didn't even want to go back there but figured it would be weird if he didn't and for all the "experience" he'd gotten from Scott he didn't want to out their relationship...or whatever it was to his brother. He got back to the couple and Ollie had a sly smile on his face.

"Remember, you talked to me about forgiving Honey?"

Bailey shrugged and tried to put on an interested face, but he wanted nothing more than to figure out what the hell was going on when they were around Ollie.

"Well, we've made friends. I'll admit that I wasn't planning to go as far as I did, but I heard her side and we've both missed each other so I stopped being a stubborn asshole." Ollie held his cup up like they were going to toast although he was the only one with a drink.

"I'm glad, man," Bailey said quietly. "No one needs to live their life for someone else you should do what you want to do. The chips have to fall where they may." Bailey avoided Scott's gaze even though the man was doing any and everything to get his attention.

"Oh, look," Scott waved someone over who was near the offices. Bailey just wanted to go home. It was too bad that it was only one o'clock and he had a few more hours to work. "It's Mark. He owns this dump. Mark, this is my brother Ollie," Scott said happily and sounded like he was happy Mark had saved him from certain fate... like Bailey.

Ollie turned toward Mark and froze. He didn't say a thing and his face turned a pink flush. Did he know this guy? Ollie cleared his throat and took a few gulps of the strong drink like it was water. "Ummm, good to meet you."

"Ollie, huh? That fit's you," Mark said with a knowing smirk he directed to the man on the stool next to him.

"Oooookay," Scott said slowly and tried to again look at Bailey. "Mark, could you keep Ollie company for a few minutes, I need to talk to Bailey about something really quickly."

"You sure he's safe with me?" Mark was smiling, but there was something so off about how both he and Ollie were acting. Ollie had definitely met Mark before, but where and what had happened? It wasn't the time or place to get into it since Bailey's whole happy situation seemed to be cracking under pressure.

"We don't need to talk now," Bailey said. "I'll stay here with Ollie."

"I'm a big boy," Ollie joked, although the words and the tone were good there was a look of something in his eyes. It wasn't quite panic, but it felt just as erratic. "I think I can sit at a bar for a few minutes by myself. What could happen?"

Bailey smiled at Ollie remembering how many times they'd said that. It basically was their code for 'Let it happen, it's okay'.

"Then we will return shortly." Bailey had another reason he'd not wanted to go. He was pissed at Scott and didn't want to have the argument at a place he'd have to monitor his tone. Following behind Scott blindly Bailey knew what had to be done and damn it he didn't think it would have come down like this.

The room Scott had chosen was Mark's office. Bailey looked around the room at the awards and the newspaper write ups on the walls. Doing anything to calm himself down, but it wasn't working. "You brought me back here for something so say what you need to say."

"I'm sorry," Scott's voice was soft. Bailey turned to see where he was and the man was standing right behind him, but looked a bit nervous about what to do next.

"Yeah, I'm sure, but here's the thing—we've been doing something for the last few weeks. I'm thinking I'm learning my new partner and you were still offering an experience. Weren't you?"

Scott looked puzzled and damn if that didn't piss Bailey off more.

"You don't mind us making out around here or at the house, but I've noticed how hard you try not to let things get too hot and heavy. We fuck around, but we don't fuck. I thought you were waiting for me to be ready, but the truth is that wasn't ever going to happen. The look on your face when you thought your brother knew about us told the whole story. I was ready to tell your brother about us, hell, I was ready to tell the world."

Scott opened his mouth and stepped forward with his hand up like he was going to touch him, but Bailey waved him off and moved further away.

"I'm done with this, Scott. You've had a long time to figure out if the crush you had on me so long ago could be moved to something more. I've had the same amount of time. There wasn't a day that I didn't think about you and what I thought I threw away." Bailey didn't want to look at Scott but he let his gaze pass over him quickly. He looked beat, tired and worn. It was like Scott was the personation of all the things Bailey felt inside.

"There are reasons I don't want to tell Ollie," Scott's words trailed off and Bailey turned to him willing and wanting to hear something that would make sense of this.

"Okay. What are they?"

Scott cleared his throat. "He doesn't want me to be with you. When you left, he was mad at everyone for taking his best friend, the one he had all the plans with, the one he loved like a brother and he was in a very dark place."

"I'm sorry that things happened the way they did."

"No. I'm not finished." Scott moved closer, but Bailey stood his ground, and he made sure the man knew he was in no mood to be touched. "I promised that I wouldn't be with you. Every time I'm with you I feel like I'm betraying him, but you're hard to resist."

"When your brother is there I'm quite resistible." Bailey couldn't believe that it was just this that was keeping them apart. "I'll tell him that I started it. It's true and it takes you off the hook."

"Ollie didn't talk to me for five months after I drove you away. I don't think he's talked to Honey at all since then. If he has then it's only harsh words and anger he gives her. I don't have any other family beside him and my mother and I don't want to go down that road again."

"So to appease your brother you'll slink around in the shadows with me, but nothing more?" Bailey was thinking of this closeted existence and it sounded so stifling. He took a deep breath and then let it out. "I respect what you're saying about your brother."

The deep breath from across the room sounded like he'd held it for a while, Bailey looked at him and wondered how he'd be able to make it without him after learning so much about himself and his desires with him.

"But I won't live like that. I appreciate all the experience, but now I guess I'm on my own to actually live life." Bailey walked toward the door. "I'll make sure to keep your secret from your brother, because we sure as fuck wouldn't want him to know we could have been really happy together."

Chapter 18

SCOTT FELT LIKE ALL the air left the room when Bailey walked out. He was standing in the middle of the room wondering what he was going to do. Bailey was pissed and he'd not seen that anger directed at him ever. It wasn't the hot anger that led to heated debates and resolution it was the cold slap of anger that came with being done. He didn't blame him. Who wanted to be someone's secret? No one.

Walking back out onto the bar floor everything seemed tainted. The jovial mood of the place was grating on his nerves. He was used to looking at Bailey across the crowded room and sharing a knowing smile or a heated glance, that shit made his whole day. One glimpse at Bailey and he knew that shit was over. He stood by Mark and Ollie listening to them, but he could see the tenseness of his shoulders.

"There he is..." Ollie said when he noticed Scott edging around the perimeter of their group. "I was just thinking we should all get together."

"All meaning who, exactly?" Scott kept his eyes on Bailey, who was looking everywhere but at him.

"I was thinking me, you, Bailey, Honey and...and Mark if he wants to come. We haven't done anything in a long time." Ollie had been drinking quite a bit from the flush on his face and the drunk happy volume of his voice.

"When did you start talking to Honey?" Scott asked as he sat on the bench.

"Just recently. Bailey convinced me that I've been an ass and I've drawn this out way too long." Ollie looked at all of them, but when his eyes landed on Mark they were decidedly... warm?

Was it him or was Ollie making goo-goo eyes at Mark? He must be more delirious than he thought.

"Also the room I had for you has cleared out. My makeshift family went back to her ex-boyfriend and it's ready for you if you want it," Ollie said to Bailey.

"I thought you and she had a thing and I thought her boyfriend was abusive." Bailey was cleaning glasses as he spoke and Scott wanted to get his attention and beg him not to take the space, if only the man would look at him.

"Sort of and he was...probably still is but that is what she wanted. You can't choose who you love, I guess. I wish her nothing but the best." Ollie took a deep breath, drank down the rest of his drink and set it back on the counter. "So, you in or are you too comfortable with my little bro to leave? Not an issue if you are. I know how you like to plant yourself and stay."

"No," Bailey glanced over at Scott then. "I think that would work well."

"Wait!" Everyone near them turned and Scott realized how loud that came out. Bailey stopped cleaning the glasses and stood up.

"What, Scott?"

"Don't you want to think this through?" Scott had always wanted to pay his brother back. The times he'd saved him in school and made him feel safe and included at home meant so much to him, and he didn't want to let him down. His brother had asked for one thing and he'd pretty much fucked it up. Now he was fucking it up with Bailey too.

"What's to think through? Your brother would love to have me stay with him and don't we all want what will make Ollie happy?"

Scott looked over to what his brother would think of that and noticed he was paying more attention to Mark than to their conversation. "Come on, Bailey."

With only the lift of one eyebrow Bailey told him how ridiculous the man thought he was. "I'm trying to do what's best for everyone." Bailey acknowledged someone at the end of the bar who needed a drink and left to take care of it. Scott followed him down to the other side.

"Staying with me would be best for everyone," Scott said when he got to the spot Bailey was pouring a drink.

"I'm keeping secrets for you, living out Ollie's post-high school dreams of living together and eating my own fucking heart out. I don't know what you want from me. I'm not the guy you built up in your mind. I'm just a dude who fell for his best friend's little brother and apparently I'm the one who has to suck it up."

"I'm going to tell him one day soon. If he thinks his thing with Honey is long overdue, maybe he'll forget about the promise he made me commit to." Scott was hopeful Bailey would like that idea but one look at his stormy face said it wasn't enough.

"The fact that you don't want to tell him says a lot to me. I don't want to get in between you and your brother but I also don't want to be with a guy who won't fight for us. Your brother isn't going to be our toughest challenge, I wouldn't think, but if we're going nowhere if there's no trust and there's no confidence in each other." Bailey walked away to deliver his drink to the customer and stopped on his way back. "I think we should just stop for now. I'm tired, you're frazzled and this was something you thought was going to be short term and I'm making a mountain of a mole hill."

"That's not true. I've loved you all my life. I've wanted nothing more than what we shared these last few weeks. You don't get to degrade my feelings for you because I don't want to go against my word." Scott stood up and walked down to the end of the bar where his brother was and watched Bailey slowly make his way down to where the odd couple of Mark and Ollie sat.

"Ollie I have to say something."

"Okay," Ollie said, turning toward Scott.

"I've had a thing for Bailey for most of my life."

Ollie put up his hand in the universal sign of stop. "I know this, Scott."

"I know you know this, but that didn't stop you from making me promise not to ever get involved with him. I love you and when you thought I'd driven your best friend away you couldn't have made me feel any worse than I did. I made a promise that I didn't think through."

Ollie looked at Bailey. "I was an asshole when you left, man. I was so angry at you for leaving that I took it out on everyone. In all the years you'd been gone, I thought I'd gotten over it, but I didn't really realize what I'd done to myself or others with all this anger until I really sat down and talked to Honey."

"I understand, Ollie and I'm sorry that I left everyone high and dry because I was only running from myself." Bailey playfully punched Ollie's arm. "But I'm back now and I'm done running. I am who I am. Win, lose or draw."

Scott thought those words were from him, but he appreciated that he wasn't going to let Ollie in on his betrayal. "Bailey and I are together." Scott said so fast he wondered if anyone heard him. "I know I made a promise to you, but I love him. I always have. Even though he's new in this lifestyle and I wanted to let him get experience in his own way with different people I'd rather have him for myself."

No one said anything and Scott looked at the faces of the most important people in his life waiting for something…anything. It was Bailey's deep chuckle that hit him first.

"It's about fucking time." The smile on Bailey's face gave him the courage to look at his brother. His only brother. The one he'd broken his word too.

"I'm sorry I made you make that promise and I'm sorry for any guilt you felt as you did what you were going to do anyway." His brother elbowed him and he returned the gesture.

"Okay, since we're all now happy and gay let's drink to that," Mark said on the other side of Ollie.

"Well, we aren't all happy and gay," Scott said with a frown wondering why he'd say something like that.

Ollie looked into his drink. "I don't think that's true, some of us are happy and bi."

Epilogue

"SO ARE WE REALLY GOING to do this?"

Bailey looked over at Scott and smiled. Would he ever get used to the man lying next to him? Probably not.

"Did you figure out what we're making for our dinner with friends next week?" Every Wednesday there was a dinner for Mark, Ollie, Honey, Scott and himself in one of their homes. This week it was Ollie's turn to host.

"I'm not talking about that." Scott rolled on top of Bailey and straddled his waist. "I'm talking about us getting married."

"Oh, that," Bailey said all nonchalant as he pulled Scott down for a kiss. "I know you have recently turned your thoughts around about commitment and whether we are married or shacked up for the rest of our lives you're the man for me."

"When you took me to your parents' house and told them about us I don't know who was more shocked." Scott put his head on Bailey's chest.

"I think you were the most shocked. I'm pretty sure my parents have suspected for a while, but just waited for me to come out to them." Bailey rubbed up and down Scott's back and ended each cycle squeezing the man's ass and thrusting his hard cock into his belly. "Aren't you happy you took a chance and broke your rules for an experimental straight guy?'

"I am, each and every day. Aren't you glad you came home and ended up in my house?"

"It didn't matter who's house I turned up in. I'm exactly where I was heading for. I came back for you."

"Oh really?" Scott appeared to not have thought of that by the expression on his face and Bailey was glad to shock him a bit. "Who's turn is it?" Scott always asked that question and Bailey never knew why. It was always his turn to receive and he always loved it.

"It's mine."

"Not today." Scott rolled off Bailey and took off his pajama pants.

"Have you been laying here all lubed up and ready for me?" Bailey was shocked. He'd known when the man had gotten up early he'd been up to something, but he'd never thought it was this.

"I have." Scott's smile was giddy and Bailey didn't want to do anything to mess it up but he had to say something.

Bailey brought Scott down on top of him and gave him a soft kiss. "I don't want to do this if you're feeling like you have to or you should do this for me. I enjoy everything we do and if I never top I'm okay with that. I don't know if you've noticed, but I'm a pretty awesome bottom."

"I have noticed that." Scott nuzzled the hair on his chest.

"Okay then, what's all this about?" Bailey wanted to get this conversation started because Scott was already stroking his cock through his boxers and they'd missed their play session last night so he was ripe to come.

"I told you when we started that I rarely bottom and it's true, but that doesn't mean I don't like it and I've been sucking and stroking this cock for a while. I want to feel what it can do when it's inside." Scott looked up at him and then looked concerned. "What's the matter?"

"Well, I've never done this and I don't want to hurt you."

"We will go slow to start and I'll tell you when I want it harder. Just like you do for me. Also, I'm not a wilting flower I can take this," he said, grabbing Bailey's cock in a tight grip. "And love it, but for you, your first time and your nervousness to 'hurt' me, I'll just take it myself."

Bailey loved that Scott still directed the action as he kissed Bailey hard. Poking his tongue into his mouth and drawing his out to play.

"I know you're primed. You were practically grinding against my ass when we slept last night, which may be the reason why I'm roaring and ready to be fucked this morning." Scott moved to his hands and knees as he helped Bailey get his boxers off. They'd been without condoms since they were both checked at the doctors a month or so ago. It was freeing and so damned hot.

Scott reached over Bailey to the table and got a bit of lube to put on his cock and he sat there trying to concentrate on not being overly excited.

"Are you ready, Harry?"

"Oh, man...that's a way to get me to calm down. Ugh. Don't call me that."

Scott's smile told him he knew what that would do and at least he'd be able to fit into the man's tight hole with a few pumps to spare, but watching the man stand above him and then straddle down was revving him right back up to where he was.

"You look amazing right now." Bailey couldn't hold back the words that burst from his mouth and was almost embarrassed by them as they didn't really say things like that to each other, but at that moment it was the truest thing he'd ever spoken.

"Thank you, Bailey." Scott brought himself down slowly as he apparently got used to the stretch. Bailey had seen the toys his lover had in the bedside table and they were no match for what he was preparing to sit on right now.

"Oooooh, wait... wait... wait." Bailey said, holding up his hands.

"What?" Scott chuckled a bit and Bailey could feel that in the way of a tighter grip around his cock.

"Ummm... I don't know. Is it supposed to feel that good?"

"Yes." Scott worked Bailey's cock in little by little until he was fully seated. Then he started to move. Sliding all the way up and all the way back down.

There was no way he wanted to feel all this wonder alone, so he reached for Scott's bright red cock and stroked at the same tempo that Scott was moving up and down on him. The more excited Scott got, the faster he rode his cock.

"I'm going to need you to come soon, baby. I'm not going to last much longer."

Changing his angle Scott dropped down on his cock hard twice before blowing his load all over Bailey's chest and he was so grateful. The depth of Scott's drop onto his cock and the tempo didn't stop, but Bailey was so wound up he couldn't tell Scott to slow down.

Scott reached behind him to fondle his balls and his climax hit hard. Wave after wave of pleasure rolled over his body and it didn't feel like it was ever going to stop. He shuddered and moaned again and again as Scott fell against his body moving so his cock was in the air cooling in the breeze.

"Holy fuck," Bailey said not able to put into words what that did to him.

"I know. That was amazing. We may have to do that more often."

"Scott, you know I just basically laid there and did nothing so I can barely take credit for that being amazing." Bailey moved Scott so he could see his face. "I'm sure you're just saying that, but don't worry, I'm going to work on it and get better."

"It may have been your first time and you may be thinking about other people who have come before you, but I can honestly say that is the best it's ever been."

"Why is that?"

"Because they weren't what I'd always wanted. They weren't you."

Bailey didn't know what to say to that because it touched him so much so he just hugged Scott a little tighter.

"I love you too, Harold Bailey." Scott snuggled into Bailey's embrace with a sigh.

"I'm so content I'm not even going to fuss about you using that name."

"Looks like I figured out a way to keep you quiet and content."

"Just being with you makes me content, but I'm never going to turn that down." Bailey had just woken up but now he was ready for more sleep. "Stay home and play house with me."

"I think that's a great idea. Let me get something to clean us off." Scott tried to get up but Bailey didn't let him go.

"I'm not ready to let you go. Just lay here for a while longer."

Scott settled back against him.

"I've always loved you, Scott, I'm just sorry it took me so long to stop running and figure it out."

"We're here now and you're mine."

Bailey smiled and shook his head. He enjoyed the fierceness of Scott's tone. "Anything you say officer."

About the Author

LL Dahlin enjoys making love...one story at a time. A writer of contemporary romance as Leela Lou Dahlin she's branched out into one of her favorite Genres Male/Male contemporary romance. Mother of 5 amazing children and RN Case Manager for high risk pregnant moms by day and writer by night...you can find her on social media listed below. Stop by to say hello or tell her your favorite joke.

Links as LL Dahlin

Email

LLDahlinAuthor@gmail.com

Facebook

https://www.facebook.com/LLDahlinAuthor

LL Dahlin's Penthouse - Street Team

https://www.facebook.com/groups/506864133048287/

Twitter

https://twitter.com/DahlinLL

Website

https://dahlinbooks.com/

Other Books By L.L. Dahlin

The You I Knew
The Closer I Get To You
Co-written with Draven St. James
Coming in July
He's No You

Printed in Great Britain
by Amazon